Caitlin O'Connell had fought long and hard to make her wish come true—to be a nurse. No one had believed that with her disability she could do it, but she had finally achieved her ambition. And now, ten years later, the doctor who had encouraged her dreams reappeared in her life . . .

Kate Ashton was born in Scotland. She was brought up in England but returned to Edinburgh to train as a Registered General Nurse, specialising in ophthalmics. After spending some years on the staff of one of the professional journals for nurses, she decided to write independently from home. She says that writing Doctor Nurse Romances gives her the pleasure and privilege of sharing both the real world of nursing and her dream-world.

Dear Dr Sassenach is Kate Ashton's fourth Doctor Nurse Romance.

DEAR DR
SASSENACH

BY

KATE ASHTON

MILLS & BOON LIMITED
15-16 BROOK'S MEWS
LONDON W1A 1DR

*First published in Great Britain 1987
by Mills & Boon Limited*

© Kate Ashton 1987

*Australian copyright 1987
Philippine copyright 1987*

ISBN 0 263 75763 3

*Set in Monotype Times 10.5 on 10.6pt.
03-0687-53213*

*Typeset in Great Britain by
Associated Publishing Services
Made and printed in Great Britain by
William Collins*

CHAPTER ONE

CAITLIN O'Connell overslept that morning—which would have been bad enough; it was only her second week at the new hospital and she hated to be late. But Caitlin was superstitious, and she had never yet had a good day after oversleeping.

Then there was the matter of her necklace: the little silver shamrock that Mary had given her to bring her good luck. The chain had suddenly snapped last night, just as she was getting ready for bed. As if to reverse fate she took the little charm out from beneath her pillow straight away and put it in her purse. She would find a jeweller and have it mended today, after she came off duty.

She hoped Mary would be okay. She would be starting her staffing post too today. Caitlin pictured her best friend as she had last seen her, when they had read their names posted up side by side on the pass list.

So much had happened since then; Caitlin had begun a whole new life. She showered, dressed and gave herself her routine injection of insulin. She ate some breakfast, telling herself as she hurried that it was not so drastic to oversleep now and then; although oversleeping in a foreign land, in a strange city, in a new bed-sitting-room, was certainly disconcerting.

Was it Friday the thirteenth today? No, it was Monday the thirty-first, she calculated, and there could not be a safer, more homely date than that. But Caitlin just could not convince herself that all would be well today.

'If you're not walking around ladders you're worrying,' Mary had said, and it was true. How she would miss Mary! Caitlin slipped into her navy gaberdine and let herself out into the Georgian street which reminded her so much of home.

But she was not in Dublin now. She was in Edinburgh: the capital of Scotland and the city of her dreams. She waited while a bus hauled itself up the long hill from the waters of the Firth of Forth towards where she stood shivering at the bus stop.

On Princes Street she looked out to her left at the pinnacled splendour of the Sir Walter Scott Memorial pricking the cold grey morning sky. To her right rose the Castle, dominating the street from its podium of rugged rock. And already she loved it all. She could not regret her choice.

But neither could she quite face up to why she had made it. She sat on the bus and told herself that it was her Celtic roots that made her feel so at home. Yet she knew in her heart of hearts that there was another reason why she felt that she belonged here.

It was ten years now since she had been rushed to hospital in Dublin a few weeks after her parents' separation. And ten years since her longing to be a nurse had been born. Since then she had fought long and hard to make her wish come true.

Nobody had wanted to believe that with her disability she could do it. Even if a hospital could be persuaded to take her for the arduous three-year training programme, could she stay the course? Everybody had been kind, but dubious. Her sisters, all nurses themselves, had gently discouraged her. It was such hard work, they'd said; why not choose teaching instead?

But Caitlin did not want to be a teacher. She wanted to be a nurse. At last, in desperation, she had applied to the university hospital in Dublin, sure they would refuse her as the smaller hospitals had done. But they had not refused. They had interviewed her, given her a thorough medical examination, interviewed her again—and accepted her.

And now, three happy, hard-won, hard-worked years later, here she was, a fully qualified S.R.N., on her way to her first staffing post. That she was in Edinburgh, well, that was something else . . .

'Royal Charitable Hospital!'

The bus bumped to a halt and almost everybody on it seemed to want to get out at the same stop. Caitlin was not alone in her neat navy beret, her matching gaberdine raincoat and the royal blue dress with bright white collar and cuffs beneath it.

But she stood out from the other nurses in the fresh beauty of her frank grey eyes, her clear complexion and the openness of her smile. Her newly-cut dark red hair bobbed in towards her slim neck in a glossy curve above her new starched collar and her silky fringe accentuated the fine line of her brows.

She stepped aside to let others off before her, realising that she had not yet paid her fare. Pulling her shoulder-bag free of the crush, she found her purse and took out a couple of coins. Offering them to the conductor who stood beside her, she crammed her purse back into her bag, hoping she wasn't late for work.

The conductor assessed her appreciatively, then gave her a grin and a wink, ignoring the money she held out to him.

'Off you get, hen,' he said, 'those patients'll be missing you!'

She went through the main gate and entered the hundred-year-old hospital as so many thousands had before her, rich men and paupers alike.

Next to the head porter's office stood a huge Christmas tree, still sparkling with coloured lights and tinsel and fresh a full two weeks after it had been decorated. It was the only tree in the hospital which had survived the festive season in anything like its original condition.

In alcoves regularly spaced along the main surgical corridor stood the marble likenesses of eminent surgeons and physicians who had more or less earned immortality. Caitlin was not overawed. Something in her Celtic nature told her that doctors did not triumph endlessly over sickness, and she preferred to remember patients.

She turned down a long corridor and staircase lined with gilt-lettered plaques bearing the names of people who had given money in the days when the hospital was run on voluntary contributions. But Caitlin was not unduly impressed by the lists of Royalty, bishops, lords and ladies either. She knew that all the money in the world would not buy back health for many in the wards back there. And that was why she was here.

At twenty-seven Caitlin O'Connell was no romantic lady-with-the-lamp aspiring junior nurse. She was junior, certainly—the delay before she could begin her training had ensured that. But so far as both nursing and her private life went she was far more akin to the real Florence Nightingale than to that lady's more popular image.

Behind her shy, retiring exterior Caitlin too was a discerning thinker, and her quiet manner concealed similar strong drive and purpose. She had applied these qualities of hers to coping with her own illness, and now she brought them to the care of others.

'Ah, Staff Nurse O'Connell!' the Senior Nursing Officer greeted her warmly just inside the Nursing Administration Office. 'Prompt as usual. But we'll be keeping you waiting this morning, I'm afraid. We've had that many off sick over the holiday period, but this morning it's worse than it's been. Would you mind just taking a seat, m'dear? I'll be back to you just as soon as I can.'

On any other day Caitlin might have minded being kept waiting to know where she would be relieving. It was always unsettling going to a new ward or department on a part-time, temporary basis. But this morning she was glad of the chance to sit down, catch her breath and think . . . what had she been thinking about?

She remembered waking up from a long sleep. She was in a white room. Opposite where she lay she could discern her face, a pale oval framed in darkness in a mirror above what looked like a washbasin. A bottle of clear fluid ran into a tube from a bottle hanging beside her bed and she could not move her arm. Suddenly a door opened and she had a moment of pure panic.

A man approached her bed. He was dressed in white, but Caitlin could not make out his face. He gently lifted up her immobilised arm and inspected something, then came round the bed and took her other hand in both his own.

'Hello, Caitlin,' he said.

'Hello,' she managed to return.

'How are you feeling now?'

She stared hard at his face, trying with all her might to focus.

'Why can't I see?' she blurted out in fear.

'The lenses of your eyes are a little swollen, that's all. They'll soon be back to normal and you'll begin to feel better soon, I promise.'

What a wonderful voice he had! And what a gentle touch. Caitlin felt her fear draining away. She asked how long she had been here.

'We admitted you this morning—you fainted on

your way to college. You were brought in by ambulance. Both your parents were notified, and they've both been in to see you and are coming back this evening. You were down in Casualty and now you're on the ward—a medical ward. That's all I can tell you. Don't you remember anything at all?'

'No, nothing,' Caitlin whispered nervously.

'Well, there's nothing to worry about. You know the Cottage Hospital near the college where you study? The old one? Well, that's where you are. And you're perfectly safe.'

'And . . . who are you?' she ventured.

'I'm Dr English,' he replied.

Dr English. After he left her, Caitlin lay back on her pillows and thought of Dr English. It was strange that he should be called that, because he obviously was English. There was no trace of brogue in his beautiful voice—no trace of any accent at all. And to whom might such a voice belong? Caitlin knew only that he sounded young, and that he was tall and dark-haired. But she had not been able to distinguish his features.

By the evening she was well enough to enjoy her parents' separate visits, to reassure them both and to eat a little supper. But afterwards she felt a strange sadness settle over her. She wanted to cry, but it seemed foolish to sit alone and weep. She was not the sort of girl who cried easily, but tears were streaming down her cheeks when Dr English reappeared and sat down on the edge of her bed.

'I want you to tell me all about it, Caitlin,' he said gently.

She blushed and tried to check the flow of tears. It was easy for him to say that, but she felt so confused, so lost, so friendless. How could she explain all that? How could she tell him, this stranger, how she felt at seventeen, her home divided around her, her college days almost over, her future so unclear?

'I don't know what's happening to me,' she sobbed at last.

The young doctor had to swallow hard. This child was a stranger to him, and yet he felt he knew her already. He felt he could touch the silken strands of her magnificent hair which clothed the pillow lustrously. He felt he understood her pain.

'Caitlin, you've had so much unhappiness lately. I've spoken to your parents, and I know a little of what's happened. I want you to be strong so that I can explain to you why you're here.'

She peered up at him and managed to make out dark eyes and eyebrows in a face in which youth and maturity seemed to combine perfectly.

'Caitlin, you know that your father is a diabetic?'

She nodded mutely.

'Well, sometimes the child of a diabetic parent is a diabetic too, but nobody finds out about it until they're older—the child, that is. Then they have something happen, some stress or infection or something, and suddenly all the symptoms start to show.' He paused significantly, but got no response from the girl. 'Well, that's what has happened with you, Caitlin,' he went on carefully. 'And now we have to help you to live with diabetes just as your father has.'

Caitlin was dumb with shock. All her life she had been used to her father's injections and her father's hospital check-ups. She knew like second nature the link between what he ate and how much insulin he took. She knew the need for meals that appeared on time and for careful protection from minor illness that might upset the daily balance of his life.

But now to apply all this to herself . . . it was impossible. She was young. She was fit. She had her whole life ahead of her. Suddenly the depression and uncertainty of a few minutes before vanished and her life seemed infinitely precious, more precious than anything.

Dr English seemed miraculously to have sensed her mood. He seemed completely attuned to her. The quiet white world that contained them cut them off from the rest of the hospital and the outside world, and Caitlin felt a thrill of wonder as he took her hand again.

'You're a young woman now, Caitlin, and not a girl any more. The shock of your home breaking up has probably caused this diabetes to appear in you, but it's as well that it should be found and diagnosed so soon and treatment begun. This way, if you take care of yourself, you can look forward to a perfectly normal life. You'll be able to do anything you might ever want to do.'

Caitlin watched the young doctor's face, memorising every detail of what he said. His hand still clasped her own, warm and reassuring. She believed him. She had to believe him.

Dr Jonathan English returned her gaze. He was not sure whom he was trying to reassure, his patient or himself. She was quite simply the most perfect creature he had ever seen. He had had to force himself to treat her with professional dispassion, but that was not what her lovely grey eyes, the perfect pale oval of her face engendered in him.

'You'll be able to do anything you might ever want to do,' he repeated gently.

She searched his eyes.

'Even have children?'

The doctor recoiled as if her words hurt him.

'Yes, of course,' he forced himself to reply lightly. 'Why not?'

But Caitlin had sensed something in his voice which

she did not understand—as if he was hiding something from her.

'Are you sure?' she asked, all innocence.

She paused, suddenly confused. Her hand in his went cold, then hot. She blushed and could not meet his eyes again.

'I don't really want any, actually,' she confessed in confusion. 'Not yet, at any rate. I mean, I'm a bit off the idea of marriage and all that at the moment. I want . . . I'd like a career, or something, first . . .'

Dr English smiled to hide his own confusion, then patted the girl's hand paternally, as he had seen a senior do with a discomfited patient.

'Well, there's plenty of time to think about all that, isn't there?' he said, back on a firmly professional footing once more and feeling slightly more comfortable.

He left her and retired to the relative privacy of the doctors' room, where he wondered what had come over him. He could not be falling in love at first sight with a seventeen-year-old! It was not possible. Not after all he'd just come through. He thought he was cured of women for life. Fate was too cruel. Why could it not have been she whom he'd met as a rash young medical student? But it had not been she. She still had all her life and mistakes ahead of her. He had to pull himself together.

Caitlin was thinking of Dr English. She would have to try to be brave and strong; that was what he had told her she had to be. She lay and thought over and over his words and made promises to him.

And after that there was plenty of time to get to know Dr English and to keep her promises. She soon learned that his eyes were dark honey-brown. She could soon see his face each time she closed her eyes: the intelligent eyes, the strong chin, the high cheek-bones and his lovely thick auburn hair. She learned to

listen for his step and to sense his presence before the
ward doors opened to admit him.

There was time for minutes which added up to
hours of talk with him, hours which led her to accept
and tame her diagnosis and learn to offer help and
encouragement to other young patients who were
admitted with the same thing.

And there was plenty of time to fall in love with
Jonathan English, SHO. She did not fall in love on
purpose. At first she berated herself for her infatua-
tion. But her feeling for him grew until she knew it
was real, and she began to dread the time when she
would have to be discharged from the ward.

Helping the nurses and talking to the other patients
became her pastime as she grew fitter. She began
really to enjoy the challenge of sharing her own
experience of diabetes productively like this, and one
day Dr English mentioned it to her.

'I hear you've been talking with Angela Flynn,' he
said, 'and she's much happier about her insulin injections since you spoke to her.'

'I felt the same at first,' Caitlin replied simply.

'You should be pleased at how you've helped her,
Caitlin,' he returned sincerely, 'it's a real gift you've
got with other people.'

Caitlin lowered her eyes. But inside she was glowing
with pride and pleasure that he should have said such
a thing to her, and for the rest of the day she walked
on air. There were one or two such moments with
him; just one or two, but she treasured them.

On the day she was discharged she packed quickly
and then wandered miserably down to the day-room,
unable to control her unhappiness. He found her there
as if by accident.

'Ah, Caitlin,' he said heartily. 'All ready to go?'

She cast him an angry, desolate glance.

'Yes,' she answered.

'Any plans?'

Any plans. She repeated the two words to herself and they got deader and deader. Then suddenly she knew. She looked at Dr English directly and with fresh vigour, quite innocent of the effect this had upon him.

'Yes. I'm going to train as a nurse,' she told him firmly, the plan forming itself solidly inside her as she spoke. 'I'm going to give up secretarial college and do my training. Where do you think would be the best place to apply?'

The challenge in her eyes was unmistakable. He swallowed and then replied before he realised it.

'The best hospital is the one I trained in, the RCH, Edinburgh.'

'Right. I'll go there, then,' Caitlin returned.

He stared at her in open astonishment. The memories and the feelings he had kept so firmly in check for the duration of her hospital stay were out and they were tearing him apart. She could not go there! But she would, he knew she would. And he had no hold on her. He had nothing to do with this schoolgirl, this . . . child. He forced his voice into some sort of neutrality.

'Well, good luck, then,' he said almost lightheartedly, 'send us a postcard.'

Caitlin realised that he did not believe her. She realised that he did not really take her seriously—not as a woman.

'I'll see you when I'm a Sister,' she responded grimly, 'you wait and see!'

She clenched her fists in an agony of love and loss. Why should he care, after all, what she might or might not do with her life? She was only a teenage patient with a crush on him. And he must have known plenty of those.

'Staff O'Connell? I'm so sorry to have kept you, my dear. Look, I think you'd be best for a couple of hours down in Accident and Emergency, then away up to the UYCS at midday. That'll give Sister time to speak to you before the late shift come on. And that will complete your induction, won't it?'

Caitlin nodded. It was the customary practice in many large hospitals for new nursing staff to undergo an 'induction period' during which they were rotated from ward to ward to acclimatise them. She had suffered this with gritted teeth. She had deferred to her sisters' advice to train near home in case she didn't stay the course or was sick during it, but now that she was in Edinburgh at last she could hardly wait to take up her permanent staffing post on the Unit for the Care of the Young Chronically Sick.

'Fine. Away, then, and see what you can find to do down in Casualty. My goodness, what a morning! And Auld Year's Night the night—it'll be worse tomorrow!'

Caitlin made a mental note never to rise to the lofty heights of Senior Nursing Officership. What a job! All day on the telephone—if you were in staff allocation, anyway—and everybody complaining about you behind your back.

All the way downstairs to the lower corridor, the main thoroughfare of the hospital, and along to the Accident and Emergency Department, Caitlin worried. She had only done a short stint on A & E during her training. One of the most remarkable things about nursing training was how versatile one had to be, and she had managed all right. But casualty was not her natural terrain. Her character and nursing temperament were far better suited to longer-term care, when she had time to get to know her patients and to follow their progress towards, hopefully, health and rehabilitation.

It was after eight by now and the hospital was as busy as a beehive. Porters passed her regularly, pushing their precious cargoes of patients either in wheelchairs or on trolleys, escorted by nursing staff and occasionally by a white-coated doctor. Far too many of these small cavalcades appeared to Caitlin to be coming from the far end of the corridor, where A & E was situated.

Caitlin hurried through the double swing doors which led into the huge department, past X-ray rooms on the right and recovery rooms to the left. She passed a staff rest room full of ambulance crew, then, turning left directly in front of the large outside doors which opened on to the ambulance forecourt, she entered Sister's office.

She saw a tall, thin woman of military bearing who wore her uniform as if it were the only dress she had ever known. Sister Joyce Everton was brisk. She was busy, and when she was busy she registered and dealt with everything with amazing speed and accuracy. In a second she had read the new nurse's name badge, established her age as disproportionate to her rank and decided what sort of girl she was.

'Have you any A & E experience, Staff?' she asked.

'Very little, Sister,' Caitlin admitted.

'Fine. I'll put you in Recovery—there's another staff nurse there. Come along.'

Sister whisked her along the way she had just come. In Recovery there were three large adjoining rooms, each of which could be separated off from the others by a sliding partition. Each room contained a special trolley for an unconscious or badly wounded patient, full resuscitation equipment and monitors. Oxygen was piped to each trolley head and cylinders of nitrous oxide and carbon dioxide stood nearby. Drip stands and nursing trolleys were ready laid up for life-saving procedures.

Although the main casualty area of A & E had been full of waiting patients with minor injuries in the process of being seen by a junior casualty officer, the recovery area was currently empty—much to Caitlin's relief.

'Pam,' Sister addressed the permanent staff nurse, 'this is Staff Nurse O'Connell. She's just here for the morning . . . ah, something for you, by the look of it. Watch your back, Staff!'

It was the first and last time in all her subsequent experience that Caitlin ever saw Sister Everton smile. Caitlin stepped out of the way just in time to allow a trolley pushed by two ambulance men and a policeman past. They transferred their patient to the recovery room trolley while a doctor barred access to a blonde woman and told her to take a seat outside. Sister Everton clicked her tongue disapprovingly.

'Come away this way, my dear,' she told the blonde. 'I'm sure we can find a wee cup of tea for you.'

The recovery room doors closed behind them.

'Staff, can you set up an i.v. with Ringer's solution, half strength, and get some 2.5% glucose ready too?' Staff Nurse McLean, the permanent staff nurse, requested quietly.

Caitlin set to work fast and efficiently on the job given her, while all around the trolley the other staff did the same. The patient was scarcely more than a child, she had seen. And he was comatose. She had heard the policeman muttering something about alcohol or drugs.

As soon as the doctor had ensured a clear airway, he prepared to take blood from the patient. The other staff nurse was measuring his vital signs: pulse, blood pressure and respirations. These last were deep and rapid, loud enough for Caitlin to be aware of them as she drew up glucose into a 20ml syringe on the other side of the room. She completed her preparations and

wheeled the drip stand round to where the doctor had
made room for it.

'Thanks, Staff,' Staff Nurse McLean nodded. 'We
can manage here now. Would you like to get some
nursing notes started?'

Caitlin was half relieved, half sorry to be sent away
from the scene of the emergency. Everything around
the still form of the patient had settled into a familiar
rhythm. The doctor skilfully and silently put up the
drip; the staff nurse busied herself drawing up one
medication after another into syringes nearby.

The figure on the trolley did not stir. As Caitlin
made her way from the room she noted how
dehydrated he looked, his eyes sunken and cheeks
hollow. In fact, he looked dreadful. She experienced a
familiar pang of shock—the one she always got at
first sight of a very ill patient.

A picture lodged in her mind of a small pale face
crowned by silky fair hair which fell back over the
white sheeting like a disarranged halo, and something
deep inside her rebelled at the policeman's words. This
was no drug addict, nor swallower of alcohol . . .

Sister Everton arrested her in mid-step as she crossed
the recovery room threshold.

'You'll be wanting Miss Farrell, Staff. She's taking
a cup of tea in my office. She's a wee bit shocked, as
you can imagine, but she's expecting you.'

Caitlin had no idea how Sister knew she had been
asked to admit the emergency patient. It crossed her
mind that perhaps Sister ran her huge department by
psychic communication. It was hard to imagine how
else one organised so many nurses, doctors, patients
and external emergency personnel.

Since last Caitlin had been in this corridor, all of
the previously unoccupied chairs which linked it had
filled themselves up, and X-ray staff were running a
shuttle service in and out of their rooms.

'Is it just a routine admission, Sister?' Caitlin asked, momentarily thrown by all the confusion around her.

'Certainly it is! What are you waiting for, Staff Nurse, Christmas?'

Caitlin hesitated no longer. She made her way resolutely through a knot of ambulance men near the main doors and into Sister's office. There she found herself in a small quiet world. The other occupant of it was a big blonde woman in her mid-thirties, who blew her nose, then looked up with a tear-stained face into Caitlin's.

'Good morning, Miss Farrell,' said Caitlin.

She found new admission notes in a clean folder on Sister's desk.

'Oh, you're Irish, nurse. How I do love that accent!'

Caitlin was embarrassed. She was also startled at the change in the woman, who seemed to have recovered her poise completely at the prospect of somebody with whom to talk.

'Do you mind if I ask you some questions now?' Caitlin proceeded.

'Of course not, nurse. I'll do my best to answer them—for Robbie's sake, poor child. Oh, God!'

Caitlin glanced up. The woman was passing her hand across her temples, her eyes closed. Caitlin could not help feeling that all the words, all the gestures were for effect. She tried to banish the unpleasant impression she had formed of a theatrical performance in progress.

'If you could give me his full name first,' she encouraged.

'Robert, but it seems to have got shortened to Robbie. Robbie . . . Rae.' Miss Farrell spoke the surname with cultured disdain and Caitlin noted down the name.

'And his next of kin?'

'Me. Well, I'm his mother.' The blonde smiled

distractedly. 'You might as well put me down as the next of kin. The Raes don't even have a telephone. I'm Penelope Farrell.'

Caitlin tried to reconcile the two differing surnames of mother and son. She decided to wait for elucidation calmly. The less she said, she felt, the better and clearer her nursing notes would be.

'Actually, Robbie doesn't live with me. He's adopted. He lives with his adoptive parents, on Skye. But he's been having a holiday with me, and we've been so happy together. I just can't believe this has happened!

'Can you give me the full address of his adoptive parents, please, Miss Farrell?'

Caitlin wrote down what she said. She would have to get a police message to the island of Skye.

'And how old is Robbie?' she asked.

'Thirteen.' Penelope Farrell sniffed, then blew her nose again.

'And he fell ill while he was staying with you?'

'Yes. It began last night. He was fine until just after supper, and then he said he had a tummyache. I thought he'd simply eaten too much—you know what young boys are; simply enormous appetites. But then he was sick and he just went on and on. I'm hopeless when anybody's sick. I couldn't do your job, nurse. I'm terrible! I simply fall apart . . .'

'Did he have any diarrhoea, or was it just sickness?'

'Just vomiting, I think. But he went off to bed. I heard him get up a few times in the night, but I didn't want to bother him, so I just let him be. Then this morning, when I went to wake him, he was drowsy, and there was this funny smell. I couldn't understand it.'

A funny smell! Caitlin's mind flew to the deep breathing that she had heard in the recovery room. She could see in her mind's eye the very page upon which she had read about Kussmaul breathing in her nursing textbook. She knew almost by heart the chapter on diabetic hyperglycaemia in which was described the sweetish, fruity smell of acetone on the breath as the lungs tried to blow off carbon dioxide and reduce the acid state of the blood.

'What about family history now, Miss Farrell? Have you any TB in your family? Or any other serious illness? Diabetes?'

'Not to my knowledge, nurse. My family all live to be a hundred.'

Caitlin looked up. There must be some family history; there almost always was. But not quite always. Nobody was sure of the origins of diabetes in the family, although the medical profession generally agreed that there was a hereditary factor.

'And of course I don't know how he's been health-wise all these years. Oh, it's been a terrible strain on me, nurse, wondering how he was all the time.' Miss Farrell closed her eyes again, and then, finding there was no response to her dramatic words, she changed her tack. 'I wonder if there's somewhere where I might have a cigarette, nurse? I'm simply dying for a smoke. Although I know it's a bit naughty in here.'

'I'm almost finished, Miss Farrell, then I'll ask Sister where you can smoke. If you could just tell me how Robbie was as a baby . . .'

'Oh, he was a beautiful baby, nurse. I can remember him now, lying in my arms. He was a big baby, and it was a difficult birth. I suffered terribly. He was over nine pounds—yes, nearly ten pounds he weighed. But he was a cherub, with all that lovely golden hair.' She stroked her own hair as if absentmindedly.

A big baby, but not a strong baby, Caitlin was thinking. In other words, a typical diabetic baby.

'Thank you so much, Miss Farrell. Now, we'll try to get you a smoke, shall we?'

Caitlin opened the door of Sister's office straight into the face of an oncoming doctor. Behind him bustled Sister Everton.

'I'll admit him to UYCS, Joyce, and we'll assess him further there . . . Good God!' Jonathan English gasped. 'What the hell . . .?'

His eyes held those of Caitlin O'Connell for a full second. Then he caught sight of the other woman.

'What . . .?' He turned abruptly to Sister Everton.

Caitlin stood holding the door open, horror, shock and astonishment rooting her to the spot. Jonathan English looked as though he had seen not one but two ghosts. The colour drained from his face and then flooded back into his cheeks as his eyes met those of Caitlin again.

Sister Everton cleared her throat officiously.

'Well then, that's fine, Dr English. And Staff Nurse O'Connell here can accompany the patient as she takes up her appointment on the Unit at midday. So that suits everyone. Are you feeling better, Miss Farrell?'

Penelope Farrell was regarding the doctor with a mixture of amused interest and haughty pride in her expression. He switched his attention to her slowly, almost unwillingly, and his colour changed again. His gaze froze and his eyes narrowed almost imperceptibly. Caitlin shivered.

'Dr English is one of our consultant physicians, Miss Farrell. He's just been in to see Robbie next door and he'll be looking after him upstairs for a wee while until we're quite sure what's wrong. Okay, my dear? Staff Nurse O'Connell, staring doesn't suit you! Get along back to Recovery. Take these notes. Staff Nurse McLean will help you with the patient and I'll send two porters along with a trolley right away.'

CHAPTER TWO

So, less than two hours since she had worried her way along the main corridor towards A & E, Caitlin found herself escorting a patient back along it. But this time she was not worrying. Worrying, for once, would have to wait, and so would the shock she had just sustained. For her patient needed her now and he demanded all her attention.

He lay, still unconscious, on the smoothly-running trolley, an intravenous infusion emptying itself swiftly into his veins. He would be under intensive care upstairs for the next twenty-four hours, the first six under her specialling.

In some ways Caitlin was glad she would be arriving on the Unit like this. Nothing was worse then appearing on a ward for the first time and not being given enough to do to disguise one's newness and unfamiliarity.

The porters swung the trolley to a standstill and pushed a button beside the lift-shaft. In this old part of the hospital the lifts were huge and open on two sides to the blackened oily shaft. Caitlin shivered. The lift appeared, she accompanied her patient inside and the doors clanked closed behind them. At the second floor they got out and found the UYCS entrance directly beside them on their left.

Sister came to the outer doors to meet them. She was a striking figure—tall, shapely, authoritative and pretty in a classical, lasting way. Caitlin reckoned her to be a few years older than herself—perhaps thirty. She wore no rings, yet she exuded the femaleness of a married woman.

'Is this our case? Welcome, Staff Nurse O'Connell. What an introduction to the Unit! Baptism of fire, eh?'

'This side, Sister?' One of the porters poked his head around a cubicle door just inside the Unit.

'Yes, that'll do fine, Jimmy. Where's the lad's mother, Staff? Is there nobody with him?'

Caitlin handed Sister Fairfield the notes. Someone had written 'For diabetic assessment' across the top right-hand corner in bold red ink. She recognised the writing.

'His mother was with him when he came in, Sister. I left her with Dr English in A & E,' Caitlin reported. To her surprise, his name sounded quite normal on her lips.

'Fine. Then she'll be up with him soon. Staff Nurse, if you'll stay with the laddie, I'll be back in a moment. I've put TPR and treatment sheets on the bed-table there for you to begin with. If you could try to get a specimen of urine. Quarter-hourly observations until he's awake.'

She disappeared.

Caitlin quietly put the room in some sort of order around her patient. She noticed that insulin had been added to the bottle of Ringer's solution which had been put up in A & E and that the bottle was almost through. He would need a great deal of fluid to replace all that he had lost prior to his admission.

As if in answer to her thoughts a male voice behind her said: 'There's more Ringer's with 2.5% glucose to go up, Staff.'

The doctor who appeared at her side was about her own age, stocky in build, fair and extremely good-looking. His name badge read: Dr Angus Dougan, SHO.

'Any change in the level of consciousness?'

Caitlin ran her eye down the observations that she had just charted. A rapid pulse and respirations still characterised them. The pupils were reacting, if sluggishly, to her torchlight now, although she could get no reaction to painful stimuli when she pinched the child's earlobe.

'There's still no response to pain, but he's slightly higher than he was downstairs,' she said.

'I'm giving him more insulin and I'll put some more glucose in the new bottle of Ringer's as soon as his blood glucose is down a bit. It's still way up over 200mgs,' Dr Dougan replied. 'The chief'll be up to see him in a minute. Are you staying with him?'

'Yes. Until four,' Caitlin confirmed.

She suffered a long and appreciative look from the senior house officer.

'Lucky lad!' he said.

'Not so lucky, Dr Dougan,' Caitlin responded coldly.

She felt in no mood for flirtatious exchanges this morning. In fact, exactly fifteen minutes ago she had shut her private self far away inside and locked an inner door. All her energy now was directed towards looking after Robbie Rae. Everything else came second to this overwhelming responsibility.

Within the next critical twelve hours the whole disastrous inner imbalance in her patient would have to be reversed. The simple sugar, or glucose, currently swamping his blood and urine would have access to his muscles and brain again, thanks to the insulin he was now receiving. The acid circulating as a result of his liver's drastic attempts to provide energy by converting fat and protein into glucose would also be abating. He would emerge from coma. And then would begin the long journey back to healthy balanced life again.

Caitlin, attending to the bed, collecting specimens, monitoring vital functions and charting fluid input and output had all this in the back of her mind. She could care for this boy as a nurse and as a fellow patient, and she knew that should enable her to give him the very best.

Sister Fairfield bustled into the side-room and cast an expert eye over the sheaf of charts on which Caitlin had been working.

'Poor wee laddie,' she murmured. 'He's coming up—good. As soon as he can tolerate fluids orally we'll start him on half-hourly drinks—just a couple of sips to start with. How are you doing, Staff? Are you managing? Fine. Dr English will be in now to see him, and I'll look in again shortly too.'

She crossed to the sink.

'You managed to get a specimen of urine? Excellent. What is it?'

'I was just about to test it, Sister.'

Sister waited to see the results: 4%glucose and positive for acetone. She sniffed and made a face.

'That'll take some shifting. How much insulin has he had now, Staff?'

'Two doses at two units per kilo of body weight,' said Caitlin, 'and 2.5mgs of glucose in each bottle of Ringer's.'

Sister Fairfield crossed back to the head of the bed and ran her hand over Robbie's brow. 'Poor wee laddie,' she repeated.

Robbie Rae's eyes opened sleepily. Sister glanced at Caitlin, then back down at the patient.

'Just you hurry up and wake up, Robbie Rae,' she instructed him. 'You've been dozing for quite long enough!'

Caitlin smiled at the older woman. She liked her new colleague very much.

'You must have a magic touch, Sister,' she remarked.

Sister returned her new staff nurse's smile. Then she raised her eyebrows infinitesimally and bustled out of the room again. 'Oh, aye!' she muttered as she went.

'He's awake,' Caitlin heard her announce in the corridor outside.

An instant later Dr English came into the side-room. Ignoring Caitlin, he went straight to the head of the bed. For what seemed a long time he looked silently at the sleeping boy, a frown clouding his features, and then he took his hand and spoke his name.

'Robbie? Open your eyes, Robbie!'

Caitlin fixed her attention on the boy's sleeping features and watched the dark lashes flicker and open.

'How are you feeling, Robbie?' the consultant continued gently.

The boy did not answer, but looked up at the kind man who held his hand with questions and confusion in his eyes.

For a split second Dr English and Caitlin met each other's eyes and read each other's thoughts.

Dr English saw a beautiful woman in front of him. Her wonderful hair was shorter, but the new style emphasised her face. He could wonder anew at her clear grey eyes and the silken texture of her cheeks. How the memory of that face had tortured his days and made impossible his nights! She was as fresh, as perfect as she had been at seventeen. But now she was a woman.

Caitlin saw that there were threads of grey at his temples, relieving the thick darkness of his hair. She noted lines at the corners of his eyes and mouth. But he was the same—older, but still the same Jonathan whose memory she had cherished all these years. What was he doing here?

She had really come here, then, just as she had said she would. He'd known she would. He had never underestimated her, not for an instant. But what was he to do now? His gaze returned to the face of the frightened boy in the bed and his heart seemed to freeze in his chest. How was it possible that they should reappear in his life simultaneously? What was he to do?

Caitlin saw the physician's expression change to one of deep concern as he roused the child once more. She could no longer bear to be with him in a confined space, and before she properly realised why, she had excused herself and quickly left the room.

Outside in the corridor she recovered herself. She saw a student nurse just inside the Unit, checking medicines at the dangerous drug cupboard.

'Excuse me,' she said, 'I'm specialling the emergency admission. Could you tell me where the staff loo is?'

'First on your right, inside the cloakroom,' replied the girl with a brief gesture of her head. 'How is he?'

'Conscious,' replied Caitlin.

She plunged into the cloakroom, caught her breath and looked at her face in the mirror. A bright pink flush spread across both cheeks. Removing the cap which she had pinned on rather hastily in Nursing Admin, she ran cold water and splashed her face. That felt better. She drew a comb through her hair. It had been a big step to have her waist-length hair cut, but at this moment she knew it had been a right one. The woman who faced her in the mirror was not the romantic schoolgirl who had once fallen in love with her handsome hospital doctor and whom he had spurned. She was, if not quite the Sister she had boasted of becoming, then at least a grown woman and a professional person. He could not patronise her now. She pinned her cap back carefully.

'Hello!' Sister Fairfield caught Caitlin emerging from the cloakroom. 'I was just coming to tell you to go for coffee. Nurse Adrian will take over from you for ten minutes.'

'Oh, thanks, Sister. A cup of coffee would be great.'

Caitlin found coffee and biscuits laid out neatly on a small round table in the centre of Sister's office. Pouring herself coffee from the flask, she discovered that her hands were trembling.

The trouble was, two worlds had collided with the appearance of Jonathan English in the side-room a few moments ago. Caitlin's private, innermost world in which she had cherished his memory had come traumatically into contact with the outside world, the one in which she lived and worked.

She had just witnessed in reality the scene she had relived time and time again in her memory. She knew that as Robbie had gazed up into Dr English's face he had felt the same as she had done all those years ago. And she knew that Dr English had been reliving that meeting too.

Yet then it had been her hand which had rested tenderly in his. How could she forget? She could not forget. But ten years was a long time. In ten years she had grown up, and as a mature woman she had to face the truth behind her girlhood dreams. If ten years had wrought unknown changes in Jonathan—she thought about those threads of grey hair, the lines about is mouth—then the same ten had transformed her too.

She was no longer an impressionable girl, but an independent woman. She was a professional woman too. She faced the challenge of working with this man as his equal, and that was what she would do. It would cost her some self-discipline, but she would do it. As if to reinforce herself she looked at her watch and told herself her coffee break was over. She washed up her cup and dried it carefully, then returned to her patient.

Nurse Adrian was in her third year of training—she was the girl whom Caitlin had seen at the drug cupboard—and she was clearly cut out for a career in nursing administration. She had seen meticulously to everything during Caitlin's absence, but had not yet actually spoken to the patient.

Caitlin immediately rectified this. If Robbie Rae was to be roused from his dangerously low level of consciousness, speaking to him, stimulating him was essential.

'Dr English wrote him up for some more insulin i.v. at two pm and six pm, when he'll review the situation according to the blood results,' Nurse Adrian told Caitlin.

'That's fine. Thank you very much, nurse. There's still plenty of hot coffee,' she added. Nurse Adrian treated her to a haughty look. It was funny how a student nurse could treat with disdain a staff nurse, or even a Sister, if she thought she was merely a relief, without the station of her own ward or department.

Caitlin smiled wryly to herself as the girl left the room. She remembered feeling much the same herself not so very long ago.

Virginia Fairfield felt well pleased with her new staff nurse. She had seen her only briefly at interview, or rather after the interview, as she had been called away to an emergency admission during it. But the favourable impression that the O'Connell girl had created then had just now been confirmed.

Sister had not liked Caitlin simply for the compliment she had received from her. Virginia Fairfield was not easily flattered. But she had liked her for the way it had been given, the way it had betrayed the staff nurse's involvement with her patient. Staff O'Connell had forgotten rank and status, everything except that she was caring for an unconscious patient who had just opened his eyes for the first time.

Sister Fairfield liked that. And she liked the fresh

open look in the Irish girl's eyes, and her trim neatness and the unfussy way she'd coped with her first morning on the Unit.

Angus Dougan had been impressed with her too. Not that that had surprised Sister; he was often impressed by new and pretty additions to the nursing staff. But this, Sister sensed, had been different. He had felt a special quality in the new staff nurse and had been pleased to learn that she would be joining the permanent staff.

Sister Fairfield had had difficulty replacing the last permanent staff nurse who had left to have a baby. Nurse Adrian had caused some unpleasantness with her request to stay on and staff on the Unit after finals. The SNO (allocation) had found it difficult to accept Sister's reasons for not wanting the girl. But Sister did not feel that she would make a good staff nurse for the Unit—and that was that. There was no arguing her out of the feeling.

You needed a certain type of girl for looking after young people with chronic sickness; someone who wasn't too high and mighty, somebody who could treat the patients as equals. It was no earthly good pulling rank on an ill teenager or young person. They needed encouragement, emotional support and someone with whom they could share their anger and sorrow as well as their healthy rebellion and laughter.

Caitlin had the qualities she looked for; Nurse Adrian didn't. And that was that. Some time today, Sister reminded herself, she must extract Staff Nurse O'Connell from her young patient for half an hour and introduce herself properly. The Unit was no ordinary ward either. That would need special introduction and explanation. She would do that before the new girl went off this afternoon . . .

'Where the hell are the haematology results on that boy? The ten o'clock ones?

'I beg your pardon, Dr English?'

Sister Fairfield turned round from her desk to find the consultant physician addressing her back.

'I said where are the blood results on the Rae boy?'

Sister faced him squarely.

'I thought that was what you said,' she replied coolly. 'I think they're lying on your desk.'

'Well, they're not,' the doctor retorted.

Nurse Adrian, on her way past the nurses' station to the day-room, looked distantly at the person whose voice had disturbed the silence of the late morning lull. Sister Fairfield indicated her junior with a movement of her head.

'You're disturbing the staff, Jonathan,' she reproved her medical colleague gently.

'Come on, Ginny, I want those reports!' Dr English snapped back at her.

She led him out towards the doctors' room. She was rattled. What was the matter with the man? He never usually spoke to her like that, let alone snubbed her in the open ward.

In his room, she crossed briskly to the desk, moved aside a pad of blotting paper and a bundle of notes and held up two blue forms.

'Here we are—nine am and ten am reports.' She handed them to the physician.

Taking the reports in one hand, Dr English closed the door with the other.

'And what's that girl doing here?' he queried.

'Which girl?' asked Sister Fairfield in amazement.

'The Irish girl.'

Jonathan English's face was set, his jaw rigid and his voice as hard as granite.

'If you're referring to my new staff nurse, Caitlin O'Connell, she's just this morning joined the staff,' Sister responded calmly.

'Just joined the staff!' Dr English exploded. 'What

do you mean, she's just joined the staff?'

'Just what I say,' said Sister.

'Why didn't I know? Why wasn't I consulted?'

'Since when were you consulted over the appointment of a staff nurse, Dr English?' Sister's voice rose to match his. It was really too much! He was behaving atrociously.

Dr English seemed to come to his senses. Virginia Fairfield watched his face change with satisfaction. At least she had some effect on him, even if it was not precisely that which she would wish . . .

'Senior staff . . .' he muttered somewhat lamely.

'Senior staff indeed!' countered Sister, capitalising on her upper hand. 'If we were looking for a new Sister, now, that might be a different matter. But a staff nurse? Really, Jonathan! And anyway, what on earth's wrong with the lass? She's been nothing but a wee gem with your emergency this morning. And her first time on the Unit . . .'

'All right, all right, Ginny, that'll do. I've written the Rae boy up for more insulin. His blood values are down a bit, but not far enough for more glucose yet. Keep pushing fluids, oral, as soon as you can. His electrolytes are improving, but I'll write him up for more potassium, I think.'

Sister noted his more normal expression. 'And you could maybe write me up for a bit of a break, eh, Dr English, and no more words today?' She winked at her colleague.

He did not return her smile. Sister Fairfield left him staring at the desk as though he had never seen it before. What on earth was eating him she could not imagine.

Dr English was her special favourite amongst the medical staff. He was usually charming to her. He was universally loved by the patients. He was all that one could wish for in a consultant physician and his temperament offset perfectly the rather dour demeanour of his opposite number on the senior medical side, Professor Carstairs.

Virginia Fairfield frowned, then sat down at her desk at the nurses' station once more. It particularly upset her that Jonathan English should have been so rude to her this morning. For last evening, much against her usual sensible nature, she had decided that she was in love with him.

When Caitlin got back from lunch, Nurse Adrian was busy checking potassium into a bottle of Ringer's solution with Dr Dougan.

Caitlin was pleased to be back in her little world containing Robbie Rae. Lunch had been a rather lonely affair. She had gone off with the two students on early, but they had left her to join a table full of friends. Caitlin had sat alone, eating out of habit and duty, unable to fill the cavern of confused unhappiness inside her.

Nobody had spoken a word to her in the bustling canteen. She had even been able to imagine that people were avoiding her table on purpose. Paranoid delusions, she thought miserably. What's the matter with me?

'Ah, Staff Nurse O'Connell! Nice to see a smiling face!' Angus Dougan greeted her.

Actually, Caitlin had not been smiling, but the look directed at her now by Nurse Adrian made her do so.

'Nice lunch?' the senior houseman enquired cheerily.

'Fine, thanks,' Caitlin replied.

'Well, this young gentleman's feeling a whole lot better, aren't you, Robbie?'

Robbie looked wanly but curiously up at her. It was so good to see him awake and responding that Caitlin had to restrain herself from laughing out loud at his pathetic expression.

'Well, there's no need to look at her like that, young fellow. She's been taking care of you all day,' chided Dr Dougan in friendly tones.

'You can go for lunch now, Nurse Adrian,' Caitlin told the junior nurse, 'and thanks very much.'

'I'll be off for a bite too,' said Dr Dougan. 'Shame we didn't coincide, Staff Nurse—I could have shown you the staff canteen personally. Salubrious, isn't it?'

'Well,' said Caitlin uncertainly, 'you could say that.'

It was nice to speak normally to somebody. Or maybe her lunch was doing her good. Anyway, Caitlin felt better. Her patient was awake and that cheered her up. And Dr Dougan was nice. Perhaps he wasn't the usual brand of junior medical flirt after all. That would make a refreshing change.

After he left, she tidied Robbie's bed and put up a new bottle of i.v. Ringer's solution.

She said hello to him again, but he didn't reply. His beautiful honey-brown eyes regarded her solemnly and he watched every move she made around his room.

She chatted to him about everything she was doing, then sat quietly beside him while he slept, stirring only to record his pulse and blood pressure. His observations had been reduced to hourly and were stable. His urinary output was still scant, but his colour had improved and his pulse slowed down to normal. Gradually his fluid balance was righting itself.

All afternoon, Caitlin remained in her little closed world, watching her patient improve by the hour as he responded to insulin and glucose therapy. Dr Dougan popped in several times and then Nurse Adrian appeared again.

'Sister says will you go and see her. I'm to stay with the patient.'

'Fine—thanks,' said Caitlin.

She slipped out of the room and found Sister at the

nurses' station.

'Ah, Staff Nurse O'Connell, I thought I'd have a word with you about the Unit, and I wanted to catch you before you went off.'

Caitlin followed Sister through the Unit, taking in all she was told. The place was really a standard traditional Nightingale ward, with beds at regular intervals up both sides and a long gangway in the middle, but it had recently been upgraded to give more space, light and recreational room for the eight or ten patients.

'This is a unit for the stabilisation and rehabilitation of chronically ill young people, as you know, Staff,' Sister began, 'and we run it on much less formal lines than a normal medical ward.'

She ran through the currently hospitalised patients, giving Caitlin a full report on the medical condition of each. In the day-room at the end of the Unit—a lovely large airy room which overlooked a park—she was introduced to six of the eight patients.

'One of the lads is out buying clothes. He's due to go home tomorrow,' Sister explained. 'And Jamie . . . well, Jamie could be anywhere.'

Caitlin looked surprised.

'Jamie Ferguson is the Unit menace,' Sister continued with equanimity. 'He came to us eighteen months ago from Intensive Care where he'd been nursed for six months following multiple injuries sustained in a road accident. He's medically fine now. But he has other problems. His parents don't want him; they never visit. The social services are having trouble finding a permanent place in care for him. He's a wee bit strange sometimes still, from the head injuries, but he's really awfully sweet.

'I don't need to tell you he's institutionalised after all this time, and we all spoil him terribly, I'm afraid. Well, so do all the nurses in the RCH. He has the run of the hospital. He's just turned thirteen—our youngest inmate up until today. Robbie Rae's the same age, isn't he?'

'Yes, Sister.'

'Well, I expect they'll be buddies soon enough. Ah, Staff Nurse Harrison, this is Staff Nurse O'Connell, our new addition.'

'Welcome,' the staff nurse said with a brief smile. 'That child! He's been down with the electricians in the basement and he's absolutely filthy!' She continued on her flight towards the bathrooms.

Sister smiled placidly.

'That'll be Jamie,' she said. 'Staff Nurse Harrison will take over from you when you go off, by the way. I expect you've had enough for one day, eh?'

The minute she had said it, Caitlin felt exhausted. She would indeed be glad to get off duty. Her feet ached, her back was sore and her head buzzed with all the information she had just been given.

She had not been back with Robbie for more than ten minutes when Staff Nurse Harrison came in to relieve her. It was just before four and already the afternoon sky outside was darkening.

The permanent staff nurse cast her eye over the charts at the end of the bed, then installed herself confidently at the bedside.

'Hello, Robbie,' she greeted her patient. 'I'm Janet. How are you?'

She didn't seem to be the least perturbed by getting no reply, and pinched his cheek affectionately instead.

'You can go, love, if you like,' she told Caitlin.

At this, Robbie Rae lifted his head from the pillow and opened his eyes wide.

'Where are you going?' he asked Caitlin.

Caitlin shot him an astonished look.

'Is that the first he's said?' Janet Harrison laughed.

'It is!' said Caitlin.

'You wee rascal,' commented the other nurse to her patient. 'She's allowed to go off duty, isn't she?'

'I'll see you tomorrow, Robbie,' Caitlin promised, pressing his hand.

He gave her a rueful look.

'Bye-bye!' she said.

But she wasn't going to get off that lightly.

Outside in the corridor the afternoon visitors had already gathered, and as Caitlin emerged from Robbie's room to collect her raincoat from the cloak-room they were beginning to move inside the Unit. Caitlin came out to find the corridor clear but for one considerable presence.

Penelope Farrell hesitated in the middle of the corridor as if uncertain of something. She was quite a sight. She had done her hair up in an elaborate style on the top of her head and was clad dramatically in fur from neck to calf. Her elegant leather boots were highly polished, and she was surrounded by the heavy scent of French perfume.

This vision carried in her arms a huge bouquet of flowers. She also held a bag which Caitlin hoped contained more down-to-earth requirements for a thirteen-year-old hospitalised boy.

'Oh, nurse, what luck to see you! Where is he?' she declaimed.

'Robbie is in the side-room; just there, on the left,' Caitlin responded.

At that moment the doctors' room door opened and Dr English emerged. He stopped in his tracks at the sight of the two women and Caitlin thought he was going to turn back into the room, but instead he stood transfixed, a stony expression on his face.

Penelope Farrell melted; everything about her seemed to soften and yield to the man who had just appeared.

'Good afternoon,' she said, a strange intimate inflection in her voice. 'I've come in with some things for Robbie.' Her lips parted in a winning smile.

Dr English looked at her in silence. He felt as if he could strike that smile from her face. He had to restrain himself from lifting his right hand. It was like a nightmare in which Caitlin O'Connell was watching his every move like a small frightened animal; like a beautiful dark-eyed wild creature caught in a trap. Just as he had seen her first in the casualty department in the Dublin hospital.

And the Farrell woman was so damned confident, behaving as if none of it had ever happened to them both. As if she had a perfect right to be here with the boy . . .

Caitlin saw he was furious and she knew it was with her. She knew he wished her gone. She made for the door, cramming her beret on as she did so, and she did not begin to breathe again until she was outside at the bus stop.

So much for her first day on UYCS, she thought. So much for her long-awaited staffing post. And so much for her glittering future at the RCH, Edinburgh. What sort of future was there for her here now?

She passed the evening somehow and went to bed. She was so exhausted that sleep should have come easily, but it didn't. Low spirits struggled with her tiredness to produce a broody, unsettled state. She got up again and lit the gas fire and sat in front of it, hugging her knees. She had been lucky to find this bedsit.

There was so much to feel lucky for, and yet she could not banish her pessimistic mood. Scotland seemed alien. She did not feel she belonged here. She longed to speak to someone and wondered if she should telephone her old friend Mary in Dublin, but she dismissed the idea. Why disturb Mary at this time of night only to tell her her miseries?

It was probably just her usual post-Christmas blues that she was feeling, she reflected. There was always such a sense of anticlimax, almost of sadness, when the Christmas trees began to shed their needles, the decorations sagged. There seemed to be a no-man's-land between the end of the festivities and the birth of the new year which always filled her with a strange nostalgia.

Caitlin blinked into the firelight. She would write to Mary, she suddenly decided. Positive thinking! She found a pen and paper before inspiration deserted her and began a long, newsy letter. In it she told Mary about Edinburgh, about the bedsitter, about the RCH, and even described Sisters Everton and Fairfield. She wrote about anything and everything—except Jonathan English.

She tucked the letter into an envelope, sealed and addressed it. Searching in her purse for a stamp, she missed her little silver shamrock. Her heart turned over. Where was it? How had she lost it? What would happen to her now?

Distractedly, she pulled open the curtain as if to reassure herself that the world was still there. It was. A great white moon returned her sad gaze, its silver light reminding her of what she had lost.

Suddenly a firework burst into coloured stars above the chimney tops. Another followed it, and then another. Green, purple, pink and yellow, the points flickered and fell through the darkness. Then the ships' sirens began to sound from the harbours and all the city seemed to leap to life.

She realised that it was New Year's Eve at exactly the same moment as a velvety male voice floated down to where she stood from upstairs:

'Should auld acquaintance be forgot,
And never brought to min'?

Should auld acquaintance be forgot
And days o' auld lang syne?

For auld lang syne, my dear,
For auld lang syne
We'll take a cup of kindness yet,
For auld lang syne!'

Caitlin closed her eyes and they overflowed. That was what she had done to deserve all this—she had not forgotten him, or the days they had passed together so long ago.

A knock on her door shocked her into normality. She dried her eyes hurriedly and answered the call.

Angus Dougan stood outside. He was grinning broadly, a bottle of Scotch in one hand and a rather battered piece of mistletoe in the other. His amazement clearly matched her own, but was somewhat dampened by the flattening effect of alcohol.

'My God, it's Staff Nurse O'Connell!' he exclaimed with evident pleasure. 'Happy New Year, my sweet!' He held the mistletoe unsteadily aloft.

Caitlin had no time to avoid the kiss he planted on her lips, which was not brief. Finally, Dr Dougan leaned away and appraised her for the second time that day. The trouble was, this time she was wearing only a long cotton T-shirt, her favourite sleeping gear.

He smiled kindly at her deepening blush.

'I'm no' dangerous,' he asserted. 'I'm first-footing you. Ever heard of it? Don't you know anything about Hogmanay? Where have you been all your life?'

'In Ireland,' Caitlin stated loyally.

'Want a drink?'

She shook her head.

'You're supposed to ask me in, or it's bad luck.' Dr Dougan sighed deeply as if infinitely tired by all this explanation. 'Oh, hell! I'm no' up to a' this. I'm only up to the dram!' he said, helping himself to another swig of whisky.

Caitlin couldn't help smiling. She stood away from the door and he came in and collapsed into the only armchair.

There was another tap on the door and a girl of about Caitlin's own age came in.

'Hello! I'm Marian Forfar—I live upstairs. Is Angus here? Happy New Year, by the way.' She peeped past Caitlin to where Dr Dougan reclined. 'Ah!'

'Come in. Dr Dougan was just . . . er . . . first-footing me, I understand,' Caitlin told her.

'Yes, I know.' Marian rejoined. 'I told him this place had been let to another nurse and he was off like a shot. I put the notice up in the RCH,' she explained, 'after the last girl left. The landlord's always too busy to find his own tenants, and I know the noticeboard at the hospital's always fruitful.'

Marian sat down on the arm of Dr Dougan's chair and ruffled his fair hair. He closed his eyes appreciatively.

'Do you work there too?' asked Caitlin.

Marian had a nice, open face and close-cropped dark curly hair. She was tiny and slim and fragile-looking, and something told Caitlin that she was not a nurse.

'Well, sort of. Well, not yet. I'm a medical student,' Marian explained. 'Next year's my final year . . . oh, Lord!! she groaned, 'I mean *this* year. Listen, why don't you come up? I'm having a small do for New Year. Not too many people; just those from the house really. And a few . . . old favourites.' She ruffled Angus's hair anew.

Caitlin hesitated. In a way it would be nice to meet

the people who had other bedsits. But she was tired and she was on early again in the morning.

'Thanks, but I've got to get up early,' she said regretfully.

'No matter,' Marian responded. 'I'll come down and have a cup of coffee with you some time, shall I?'

'That should be really great!'

'Come on, you. We've got the rest of the street to do yet,' Marian told Dr Dougan.

He opened one eye.

Marian turned back to Caitlin in mock exasperation. 'What's your name, anyway?' she asked. 'I forgot to ask.'

Caitlin told her, while Dr Dougan retrieved his mistletoe from the floor beside the armchair where it had deposited its last two berries. He examined it rather ruefully, then stood up.

'Happy New Year!' he exclaimed with renewed enthusiasm, throwing his arms about both girls and hugging them warmly to him.

Marian and Caitlin exchanged looks, then both began to giggle. Angus shook his head in bemusement.

'See you soon,' said Marian.

'Have a good party,' Caitlin returned.

She suddenly felt as though she might really belong in this house, in this city. She closed the door softly behind them, turned off the fire and went to bed.

CHAPTER THREE

CAITLIN dropped the two squashy, whitish berries she had just picked up into the waste paper bin. She was sure that mistletoe played no official part in Hogmanay celebrations. She felt equally certain that Dr Dougan would not be in evidence on the Unit today—or not until much later, anyway.

January the first had dawned bitterly cold. She would definitely buy a furry coat, she decided, out of her first pay packet. She huddled into her anorak and descended the short flight of stone steps that led down to the street. Forty-two Cathcart Street was one of a row of gracious Georgian houses that lined the street of former family residences.

It was strange to think now that one family and its servants had once occupied each of these great houses which now housed law offices, city flats and, in the case of number forty-two, bed-sitting-rooms for six occupants. The rooms were large, lofty-ceilinged and sash-windowed. The floors were polished oak and the ceilings moulded around the central point, from which had once hung chandeliers. Caitlin, living in one room, felt she lived in regal splendour.

She walked quickly up towards Princes Street, the north-east wind biting through her several layers of clothing. There was nobody about. She saw a couple of girls whom she judged to be nurses too, heading in the same direction as herself. A lone policeman paced the shops on that side of Princes Street. On the other, the park stretched empty, bare and silent beneath the Castle crags.

Above the Royal Scottish Academy and the National Gallery, the huge Christmas tree which had been lit with silvery lights ever since Caitlin's arrival in Edinburgh leaned forlornly in the wind, its bare bulbs sadly dull. Suddenly Caitlin wanted the new year to begin in earnest. She wanted her new post to begin too, and for this to fulfil all its promise.

If old acquaintance must be forgotten, they must. She could not go on living in the past. She did not give the Christmas tree a second glance, but took the secret granite path up through the tenements towards the Royal Mile.

A couple of tramps were curled up in a pub doorway halfway up, and Caitlin's heart went out to them, sleeping out of doors in such bitter weather. What a world! She had to fight an irrational desire to give them the key to her bedsit. She remembered the Ward Sister who, early on in her induction, had told her to lay four extra places at the dinner table in the centre of the ward.

Caitlin, uncomprehending, had done so. At five to twelve four old tramps had shuffled in, sat down, and been served with plates of steaming hot soup. Afterwards, they had departed, as quietly as they had arrived, making for their park benches again.

And she thought of how a couple of the people she had admitted to the RCH had given as their 'place of abode' the Salvation Army Hostel. Glancing down to her left, she stared down the curving, dismal street of grey tenements towards the Grassmarket, where this hostel was situated. She could imagine the decent but meagre cots they offered to the poor.

This was the time of year in which the city down-and-outs died, unloved and unwanted. They came into the wards and luxuriated for a few brief days or weeks in clean beds, fresh linen and tender loving care. And then they died of the bronchitis, the pneumonia, the cerebral vascular accident, or stroke, which had brought them in.

There was so much work to be done; so many folk who needed her care. And she wanted so much to give it. She passed the Greyfriars Bobby pub, her pace quickening. A few minutes later she entered the Royal Charitable Hospital, glad to be in out of the cold, hushed, hungover city.

The night before had taken its toll. A quick glimpse into A & E as she passed showed her a department recovering from the busiest night of the year. In the demeanour of a woman being helped out by a policeman she recognised the broken dreams of the newly bereaved.

It made her feel lucky: lucky to be alive, to be working at the job she loved. Lucky to be herself. She ran up the stairs instead of submitting to the lift, and pushed open the doors of the Unit with joyful anticipation. Nothing would stop her from enjoying her new post and exploiting all its possibilities; nothing and nobody.

An auburn-haired, dumpy woman of about fifty sat alone in the corridor outside the Unit. Her head was bowed in contemplation of a coloured headsquare which she held over her lap. She was simply dressed in a brown tweed coat and stout leather shoes. She looked up at Caitlin's approach.

Caitlin met a pair of level, candid blue eyes in a face as fresh and open as that of a child. Only the lines around the mouth and at the corners of the eyes betrayed years filled not only with laughter but also with tears.

Caitlin, still in mufti, could not help asking if she could help her.

'No, Sister's been out and she's away to fetch me a cup of tea. I'm here to see my boy, Robbie Rae.'

Her voice was soft and lilting, reminding Caitlin of

the countrywomen back at home. She smiled as warmly as she could at the waiting woman, sensing her desolation and longing to help banish it.

In the privacy of the cloakroom while she changed, it occurred to Caitlin that there couldn't possibly be much more difference between the woman outside and Penelope Farrell.

She combed her hair carefully, telling herself that she was not concerned whether or not she saw Jonathan English today. She set her cap straight and pinned it on, noticing that her eyes were clearer and her skin in better condition than it had been for weeks. The upheaval of the move from Ireland was over, and last night she had slept properly for the first time in a long while.

Sister Fairfield had obviously not been up all night celebrating either, but the same could not be said of the first-year student nurse.

'Good morning, Staff Nurse O'Connell,' Sister said. 'Have you seen Nurse Adrian on your travels? No? Fine, we'll begin without her, then.' Sister sat down.

'We'll being with Robbie Rae, yesterday's new admission. Robbie had a comfortable night. His i.v. came down at six this morning. He's drinking plenty of fluids and passing urine well and his electrolytes are back to normal. Doctor's very pleased with his progress. He's having a bath just now and he can stay up for a few hours as long as we keep a close eye on him. He's for glucose tolerance test tomorrow, and we've started a twenty-four-hour collection of urine at seven this morning. He's quite a bright wee soul, but I'm a wee bit concerned how he'll adjust to his diagnosis.

'Anyway, Dr Sass'll be speaking to him today. So we'll just need to wait and see . . . Staff O'Connell, Mrs Margot Rae, Robbie's adoptive mother, is outside taking a cup of tea. After the report I'd like you to complete the nursing notes you began yesterday. She should be able to fill you in on all the details that Miss Farrell couldn't give you yesterday . . .'

The remainder of the report followed, and Caitlin took careful note of the comments on each patient. They were all such strangers to her still. All except one. And who was Dr Sass? That was a strange name. She was sure she had not heard of him yesterday.

'Did you enjoy your cup of tea, Mrs Rae?'

'Oh, I did, nurse. It was lovely!

'Now, Mrs Rae, I want to ask you a few questions about Robbie,' said Caitlin. 'Would you like to come this way? Sister says we can use her office. We'll have some peace and quiet in there.'

In Sister's room, Caitlin ushered Mrs Rae into a chair and pulled one up for herself.

'I hope I'll be able to help you, nurse. I'm that nervous and flustered this morning, what with the travelling overnight and a' that.' The older woman was close to tears.

'Don't worry about anything, Mrs Rae. Just tell me everything in your own time, and if we forget anything, well, it doesn't matter at all. Tomorrow is another day. Now, have you seen Robbie yet?'

'Not yet, nurse. They were bathing him when I came in.'

'Well, I'm sure you'll be able to see him directly we're finished here.'

'How is he, nurse?' Mrs Raw looked beseechingly at Caitlin.

'He's fine,' Caitlin responded quietly. 'He's had a quiet night and he's much, much better now than when he came in. Now, what do you want to tell me about him first?'

Margot Rae relaxed a little.

'He's such a brave laddie,' she whispered. 'I hardly know where to begin.'

Caitlin imagined how the couple on Skye must have felt when a policeman knocked on their door with the message that their boy was in hospital in Edinburgh.

'He's no' ours, ye see, nurse. We adopted him when he was a wee baby, and we've brought him up as if he was our ain. He's like a right son to us now. Then it was an awfy shock to us . . .'

'What was a shock, Mrs Rae?' Caitlin prompted gently.

'Well, when one of the laddies at his school told him he was no' our right son; let on, you know. We were going to tell him ourselves, of course,' Mrs Rae continued hurriedly, 'the minute he was old enough. But he's still a bairn in so many ways. But you know what wee places are like, nurse. People talk, and of course this school chum's faither was at work with my man about the time we adopted Robbie, and one day out it all came. Some folk canna hold their tongues. I canna understand it; not where bairns are concerned.'

'Was Robbie very upset?' Caitlin asked.

'No' too bad, as a matter of fact,' Mrs Rae recovered a bit. 'We all talked it over, you understand, him and his faither and me, and he seemed to accept it really well. But he's a canny lad wi' a guid imagination on him an' he must have sat and turned it a' over in his mind. Then one day, out of the blue, he says he wants to meet his real mother.' Margot Rae shrugged her shoulders helplessly. 'What can you do?' she asked.

'We talked it over, my man and me, and we decided to contact Miss Farrell. I'd always kept her telephone number down in London—I don't know why, rightly. We decided Robbie'd be better getting the whole thing out of his system, and not sit brooding about it, and maybe having problems with it through his teens. The "turbulent teens", as my man says. An' the bairn just coming up thirteen as it was . . .'

'And so you got in touch with Miss Farrell?'

'Aye. I telephoned from my sister's down the street one night. Miss Farrell said she'd be spending Christmas up in her cottage in the Pentlands. Well, that was where she lived when we adopted Robbie and I'd no idea she still had the place. I thought she'd sold up and gone off down south for good.'

'So you weren't really prepared for her to see Robbie?'

'Not so soon, nurse. I thought she'd maybe write and send a photo or something. But she invited the laddie down right away. We had about three weeks to get used to the idea, and I wondered if he'd really go, when it cam' to it. I suppose, if I'm honest, I hoped he wouldna' want to go.'

Caitlin glanced sympathetically at the older woman's shy frown.

'But he came down for the holiday in the end?'

'That's right. We didna' want to treat him like a baby, nurse, and my sister lives in Portobello nearby. But now I ken it was an awfy mistake letting him down alane. I don't know how I'll live with myself, nurse, really I don't.'

'You mustn't talk like that, Mrs Rae,' said Caitlin softly. 'You had a difficult decision to make and you mustn't blame yourself for what has happened. It might have been quite all right.'

'But the diabetes, nurse. It's a dreadful thing, what wi' the jags and a' that. I canna take it in, nurse, really I can't.'

'I know, Mrs Rae. But the doctor will speak to you and explain everything—and, Mrs Rae, you must believe that Robbie has a good chance of leading a perfectly normal life once he's learned to live with this problem.'

'It's the sugar sickness, isn't it, nurse? And he'll no' be able to eat sweeties ony mair?'

'Well, it's a little more complicated than that. He'll have to be careful to balance what he eats against his insulin intake. But we'll explain everything before he comes home, Mrs Rae. There's no need to be frightened, honestly there isn't.'

'Oh, I'm sure there isn't. I'm just being silly this morning, with being so tired and everything. I am sorry, nurse.'

'There's no need to apologise, Mrs Rae.' Caitlin hesitated for a second. 'I don't know if it will help you at all, but I've got the same thing that Robbie's got. I'm a diabetic too.'

She paused, surprised at herself for crossing so completely the professional gap between nurse and relative of a patient. But her doubt soon vanished.

Margot Rae looked up in astonishment from the contemplation of her headscarf, her eyes full of admiration.

'Oh, nurse, are you really? But you look perfectly . . . normal . . .' she stopped, flushed with embarrassment. 'Oh, how rude of me! Nurse, I didn't mean . . .'

Caitlin smiled.

'Don't worry at all, Mrs Rae,' she said. 'I know just what you mean. And I am normal. Well, reasonably!'

Margot Rae seemed so much easier in her mind that Caitlin stopped worrying in the least about her confidence. She was able to complete a full history of childhood complaints and illnesses, so that for the first time there was a proper nursing case sheet of background information against which to plan Robbie's care.

'That's super, Staff Nurse O'Connell,' Sister Fairfield complimented her when she had read the notes. 'You can tell Mrs Rae she can go in and see her son now.'

Caitlin's careful hours of observations, recordings and encouragement of Robbie yesterday were amply rewarded when she opened the door to show Mrs Rae into his room.

Robbie was sitting up in a chair next to his bed, dressed in clean pyjamas and dressing gown. He was reading one of a pile of pop and motor magazines which someone had brought him from the day-room, and he looked up expectantly as the door opened.

He was almost unrecognisable from the figure that had lain comatose through the preceding day. Once more in her nursing life Caitlin had a shock of pleasant surprise at the rapidity with which a young body could swing from dire illness to every appearance of health and vitality.

'Hello!' she said.

Robbie returned her greeting—then he caught sight of Mrs Rae. 'What are you doing here?' he asked her.

Caitlin was taken aback, but Mrs Rae seemed to take it in her stride.

'Hello, Robbie,' she said. 'How are you, bairn?'

'Okay,' responded Robbie sullenly.

Caitlin suddenly realised that it might be her presence which was affecting him, and quietly withdrew. She hoped fervently that everything would be well between them once they had talked for a few minutes. She realised that Robbie probably felt both annoyed and guilty at his independence being so limited and Mrs Rae having had to come down to Edinburgh. She also thought, uncomfortably, what a glamorous and spectacular 'mother' Penelope Farrell must seem to a thirteen-year-old boy.

'I'd like you to look after the boy again today, Staff,' Sister Fairfield told Caitlin when she arrived back at

the station a minute later. 'He's being controlled on
regular insulin over the next couple of days, according
to glucose level in the twenty-four-hour specimen.'

Specimens with high levels of glucose in them,
Caitlin knew, would indicate that Robbie needed more
insulin to get him over that time of the day, while
those without glucose would show that he needed a
snack at about that time. The spillage of glucose into
his urine was demonstrating exactly how efficiently the
insulin injections were controlling his condition.

'You don't have to watch him every second, of
course, but he should be got back to bed after lunch.
If you could test his urine at one o'clock, then re-start
the collection to run through until seven am again,'
Sister concluded.

'Fine, Sister,' Caitlin accepted her instructions with
satisfaction. It would be nice to look after Robbie all
day.

'Oh, and Dr Sass said he'd be down to talk to the
laddie some time this morning,' Sister Fairfield added.
'He always makes a point of spending some time with
his new admissions, explaining personally to them
about their condition. He's super that way.'

'I meant to ask you, Sister,' Caitlin remembered,
'Dr Sass—who is he? I don't think I've met him yet.'

Sister grinned broadly.

'I think you have, actually, Staff. "Dr Sassenach"
is the title bestowed on our consultant physician by
all his fans. He's English by nationality as well as by
name!'

'Ah!' Caitlin couldn't think of anything to say.

'Have you never heard of the term "Sassenach" for
an Englishman? Don't you use that one over the
water?' Sister asked with amusement.

'I don't know . . . that is . . . I've never heard of
it,' Caitlin replied, confused.

'Well, one of our erstwhile patients coined the name

for Dr English, and it stuck. He's "Dr Sassenach" to all the patients now, and most of the staff—behind his back, that is, of course. I thinks he know fine, actually, but if he does he keeps it between himself and his precious patients. He doesn't go in for that much familiarity with the staff!'

Caitlin felt herself beginning to blush and sought an excuse to leave Sister to her obviously pleasurable remarks and reflection upon the physician. For some reason, she found them difficult to listen to.

As soon as she decently could, she excused herself and got back to Robbie Rae. His mother had gone and he was leafing lethargically through a pop magazine. Caitlin checked all the recordings on his charts and made sure that they were up to date, then did his nine o'clock observations of pulse, respirations and temperature.

The door opened just as she was taking the thermometer out of his mouth, and Dr English walked in. He glanced straight at Caitlin and she recognised the same expression that she had seen upon his face yesterday afternoon. He was not pleased to see her—and that was an understatement! Perhaps he thought her a little fool to turn up here, to have acted on her girlhood ambition to work here.

Caitlin charted the observations she had just taken and looked for an excuse to leave the room. The physician had pulled up the chair that Mrs Rae had so recently occupied and was sitting close to the boy. As if he read her thoughts he addressed Caitlin, without looking directly at her. He could not bear to look at her—not until he had grown used to being almost alone with her again.

'There's no need to leave us alone, Staff. I won't be so long here.'

So Caitlin was left unable to go. She hovered around while Dr English explained to Robbie in his even, measured voice the implications of his illness, without alarm or complication in his words. As he did so, Caitlin ran over in her mind the time he had done the same for her, and she could recall every word he had said.

Once, while she stood near the window watching them, something strange struck her in the two. They seemed so close, so bound together somehow. It was an amazing gift he had as a doctor, she concluded to herself. It almost broke her heart that she could not tell him how she felt. She could hardly bear the distance he insisted on; how he was cut off from her by the intervening years. He seemed almost a stranger.

Robbie looked into the doctor's eyes, trust and belief in his own. Dr English had convinced him that everything would be all right, and he would reward the doctor with his good behaviour and his best co-operation. Caitlin could see it all in his face.

She had no way of knowing how the doctor felt, the turmoil in his heart as he spoke to this child. She did not guess what agony it was for him to be alone with herself and Robbie, or what it cost him in self-control to keep his voice so calm and his professional distance from them both.

He had watched her recording Robbie's observations, and noted that the slim, beautifully-kept fingers bore no ring. He could not believe that she was here, in front of him, and he was enmeshed once more with that woman . . .

'How are the injection sites, Staff?'

His question startled her.

'Oh, they're fine—er—Dr English. He tolerates the insulin injections very well.'

'Good. Fine. Well, I'll see you again soon, Robbie.'

Dr English stood up and came over towards where Caitlin stood next to the door. For a crazy moment she thought he was going to say something to her, to recognise their old affiliation—but Sister Fairfield popped her head in the door and gave him a dazzling smile.

'Okay, everybody?' she enquired.

Dr English returned her greeting and promptly left the room.

'Staff, I thought you might take the Professor's round this morning,' Sister said. 'It'll be good for you to get to know how he works and hear his wee stories for the first time. He's a wee bit dour—unlike our canny Sassenach—but you'll get used to him soon enough.'

'Fine, Sister. What time does he go round?'

'Oh, about eleven. But it takes an eternity. You'll no' be through until lunchtime. I'll keep an eye in here.'

Caitlin had mixed feelings about leaving Robbie, but was glad for the diversion.

'And I'll phone Admin just now, before the round, to see if that girl Adrian has rung in to report sick. She still hasn't phoned in to the ward. I just cannot make her out at all,' Sister added.

Caitlin got back from lunch at one as usual. One of the very few concessions that her diabetes demanded in the context of work was that she had to have her meal breaks regularly so that her morning dose of PZI and Lente insulin kept her blood sugar stable all day.

Sister Fairfield had been very matter-of-fact about the business, and once the initial arrangement had been made it was not alluded to again. Caitlin much appreciated this. It made her feel secure and unremarkable.

She took a specimen from the sample of urine with which Robbie had just presented her, then added the remainder to the collection jar.

'Do you want to watch me test this before you hop back into bed, Robbie?'

'Okay,' he agreed. 'Why do you have to test it?'

'We have to see if there's any sugar or acetone in it,' she explained, 'because if there's too much you'll need more insulin, and if there's none we'll have to give you a snack.'

'I could do with a snack—I'm a starving!'

'I suppose you're always starving?' she replied.

'Funny you should say that, Nurse O'Con, 'cos I am.'

Caitlin decided to ignore the new nickname in view of what Sister had said about the informality of the Unit. Beside, she reflected somewhat grimly, she was in good company.

'Do you know what acetone is?' she asked, setting test-tubes upright in the rack.

'No idea.'

'It's what ladies use to remove their nail varnish with.'

'Really?'

'Really,' Caitlin smiled.

'What's it doing in my pee, then?' Robbie wanted to know.

'It's produced by the liver when it's trying to turn protein into energy.'

She dropped five drops of urine, then ten of water into a tube, then added a Clinitest tablet. She set the rack straight in front of Robbie.

'You can tell me how much sugar there is,' she said. 'You have to match the colour this turns to those on the chart on the side of the Clinitest bottle.'

Robbie studied the spectacular little chemical display in the test-tube with interest.

'That's pretty,' he said as the colour changed from blue through sulphurous yellow to burnt orange. 'Four plus—that's the top score. Is that good or bad?'

'Neither,' said Caitlin with equanimity. 'Now we'll see how you are for acetone.'

She dipped a test stick into the urine sample and once more handed Robbie the jar with the colour code on the label.

'Negative for acetone. No nail polish remover. What does that mean?'

Caitlin explained, as simply as she could without using too many long words.

'So you'll perhaps need a little more insulin,' she concluded. 'It seems complicated now, but by the time you go home all this will be sorted out and your insulin requirements will be fairly stable. We'll teach your mother to help with your injections and test your urine and everything . . .'

'She's not my mother!' Robbie interrupted with unexpected ferocity. Caitlin started.

'Well, Robbie, I meant Mrs Rae. What do you usually call her?' she asked gently.

'Nothing. She's not my mother!' the boy insisted.

Caitlin felt this was no moment to remonstrate with him. She needed time to think.

'Well, you can hop back into bed now, Robbie,' she said. 'If you have a rest, I'll be back in to see you in a little while.'

She tidied up and left him. But she was ill at ease, and her spirits seemed to sink lower and lower as the afternoon wore on.

It was good to get out of the hospital and into the fresh air. Caitlin filled her lungs, only to gasp. It was still bitterly cold. She set off purposefully in the direction of Princes Street, trying to erase the memory of Margot Rae huddled in the corridor as she left the Unit exactly as she had been when she came on.

There was no justice in the world. Why should

Robbie Rae treat his adoptive mother so badly when she was so obviously devoted to him? Caitlin frowned at the memory of Penelope Farrell breezing into the side-room a few moments ago. It's not for me to judge, she thought over and over again. But then the feeling that it wasn't fair came back even more strongly.

She decided that she would do something different and not go straight back home to brood over things. A bus approached marked 'Cramond' and she recognised the name as that of a place she had marked on her map for visiting. She hopped on board and upstairs to the front seat, pleased with herself for the change in routine.

At Cramond village she got off the bus and hurried down in the direction of the strand, hoping her memory of the map served her well and that she would get a glimpse of the sea before it got dark. The little narrow road, flanked by stone cottages, was deserted.

She emerged quite soon on a broad esplanade, a river to her left and almost directly in front of her a long stone pier with a lighthouse at the end of it. Screwing up her eyes, she thought she saw a figure far out along this, but then she shifted her attention back to the shore.

The sea that lapped the pebbly beach was steely grey and inhospitable. Gulls swooped low above the icy waves, snatching at the water and then wheeling high again, uttering their strange, sad cries.

Caitlin shivered. She had been unprepared for the desolation of this spot. To her surprise, a definite figure emerged from the cottage on the opposite bank of the river and gestured to her. She waved back, uncertain of what he meant. He came down to the river and pushed out in a boat—the ferryman! Caitlin had not meant to cross the river, but she set off towards the landing stage. Having hailed him, however

inadvertently, she did not feel able to refuse his offer
to take her across.

She paid the other side then stepped off into the
brownish grass. Ahead, along the beach path, were
dunes, bare trees and solitude. The light was fading
rapidly. Caitlin decided to walk briskly for ten minutes
along the path, then retrace her steps.

At first she felt nervous, but soon the peace and
quiet calmed her and she began to enjoy her little
adventure. It was the first time in days that she had
forgotten work.

After ten minutes by her watch, she came to a fork
in the path, hesitated, then impetuously took a turning
down towards the sea. It let to a small cove,
surrounded by high rocks and completely inaccessible
from right or left. Across the sea she could see the
gathering dusk over Fife, and high above the moon
appeared suddenly and surprisingly in a gap in the
clouds.

Caitlin set off back unwillingly, yet knowing that
she must, in the direction of the village. Everything
was very quiet and still, and when she got into the
woods her steps speeded up. The first flakes of snow
began to fall and blow across her face as she reached
the river. The ferryman must have been looking for
her, for he came out of his cottage as she arrived.

'Just in time, lassie,' he remarked ominously, punting
them skilfully across the water.

Once on the other side, Caitlin had difficulty in
seeing where to step out. It was suddenly almost
completely dark. The moon had disappeared and great
flurries of snow obscured the view. Snow clung to her
face, freezing her cheeks and almost blinding her. She
stumbled and almost fell.

'Here, give me your arm.'

Dr English had been to his old haunt and thinking-
place along the old pier at Cramond for the third time

recently, but he still could not sort out how he should
proceed. It was all such a mess—with Penelope and
the boy. And Caitlin O'Connell. Caitlin. He had stared
out at the sea until the wind froze him to the spot and
whipped tears from his eyes. He did now know what
he could do about Caitlin. He offered the woman his
arm before he recognised her, and then it was was too
late.

'My God!' he muttered beneath his breath.

'Dr English!'

But by then her hand was tucked under his arm
and they were stumbling side by side towards where
he had left his car beside the beach cottages.

She needed his solid strength to shelter her from the
worst of the wind and driving blizzards, and she
leaned against him gratefully, a surge of warmth and
certainty suffusing her cold limbs and face. Surely he
would speak to her now?

He held her close to him, putting off the moment
when they reached his car and he would have to let
her go. No words came to his lips. He held her arm
as if he never wanted to let her go, while the knowledge
that he must do so tortured him. A mad idea came to
him that he would keep her here tonight. Just book
them into the inn and stay—tell her everything—but
instead he led her to the car.

They got in and he removed his gloves and found
his keys, then turned one in the ignition. He sat and
stared motionlessly out of the front for a while, then
spoke without turning his head, wearily.

'I never expected to see you again, Caitlin. Especially
not . . . like this.'

A thousand things filled her mind to say, but nothing
came out. She fixed her gaze on the bunch of white
heather that adorned the rear-view mirror and
wondered numbly what sort of luck it was that had
brought them back together again like this.

The engine started up and he reversed, then drove slowly up the hill, waiting for the condensation to clear on the windscreen.

'Where do you live?' he asked at last.

'In the New Town,' she responded quietly. 'At Cathcart Street, number forty-two.'

They got there and he stopped the car. She got out, thanked him, and fumbled for her keys. Her heart thumping, she let herself into the house, unable to face hearing him drive away.

But he did not drive off straight away. He sat for a few moments confronting his feelings. It was the first time that he had done so quite so honestly and it hurt. Ten years ago, he told himself, he had been a coward—a coward and a hypocrite.

He had preached to himself about the professional rights and wrongs of falling in love with a patient. He had reminded himself of how young she was. And he had managed to convince himself that it was a good and noble act to let Caitlin O'Connell go.

He could not lie to himself any longer. It was fear that had led him to pretend he did not know how she felt. Fear that had stopped him from telling her to stay in Dublin; the fear that his rejection at the hands of Penelope Farrell had left in him. Penelope Farrell. How he hated her!

CHAPTER FOUR

SHEER exhaustion ensured that Caitlin slept soundly for twelve solid hours. But the minute she awoke it was to worry, and to the memory of Jonathan's transformed face.

In the hospital she had not noticed how haggard he looked, but under the sodium lights last night he had looked positively old. Her heart aching, she wondered where was his shy smile and the quiet assurance in his eyes.

And what had he meant by the words 'not like this'? They tumbled over and over one another in her mind until they were meaningless.

Perhaps he meant their old patient/doctor relationship. Perhaps he couldn't cope with discovering her to be his professional equal on the staff of the RCH. Was that what had shocked him into such defensive behaviour towards her?

January the second, she thought in desperation. Not too late for a New Year resolution. I shall not . . . she began defiantly to herself . . . I shall not dream, speculate or . . . concoct fantasies around this man whom I once knew. I shall confine myself to working beside him in a dignified manner and concentrate on excelling in my new job.

Well, she reflected as the door of number forty-two swung closed behind her, that should keep me good and busy!

Staff Nurse Harrison had gone off on the holiday she had been planning ever since Caitlin's appointment. Sister was on early and Caitlin would be in charge of the Unit after she went off. The Unit felt relaxed and calm when Caitlin and Nurse Adrian sat down for the afternoon report, and Caitlin hoped it wasn't the calm that preceded a storm.

'We've admitted two new patients on Dr English's side,' Sister Fairfield began, 'but they've both been in before, so they know the ropes. Davy Selkirk is twenty-five, Church of Scotland, Hodgkins' Disease. He had radiation therapy last summer when he was last on the Unit and he's been admitted following a relapse over Christmas. He's suffering from a mild upper respiratory infection just now, and we'll maybe start him on steroids and more chemotherapy later in the week. He's for observation and rest, though he can be up and about with care . . .'

Caitlin tried hard to concentrate. The other new admission was a haemophiliac who had been bleeding for a week. He was in his early twenties and was normally controlled well at home on his own supplies of anti-haemophilic factor, but he'd been kicking a football about with some friends and fallen hard, causing bleeding into the knee joint which had not stopped since.

Nurse Adrian took copious notes. In between jotting things down, she examined her bitten fingernails. Caitlin felt distracted by her. She fidgeted continually and kept casting sidelong glances at Caitlin with her rather tired greenish eyes beneath their dark fringe of lashes. She made Caitlin feel distinctly uncomfortable.

'Robbie Rae is progressing well,' Sister continued. 'He took four doses of regular insulin yesterday. His twenty-four-hour collection is completed, as is the glucose tolerance test begun this morning, and he's up and about. Staff, I'd like you to see to him today, plus the new admissions and the other two of Dr English's patients. Nurse Adrian, you can oversee the Professor's patients.'

Sister went through Professor Carstairs' patients, then sent Nurse Adrian off to begin fasting one of them.

'Staff Nurse O'Connell, there's one other thing. The clinical nurse for community care is coming up from the Renal Unit to see Linda Dale, our chronic nephritis case. Sister Duncan rang me to say she wanted her community care nursing specialist to see her about how she'll manage after discharge from this Unit, and to tell her the arrangements for liaison with the Renal Unit too. I'd like you to speak to her when she comes up. I'm thinking of trying to set up a similar support scheme for our discharged diabetics.

'The community care isn't too bad at present, but it could be much improved. I'd be glad to hear your opinion of how you think such a scheme would work from the patient's point of view—well, from both sides, really, both professional and personal.' She gave Caitlin a brief, warm smile.

It was a compliment to be taken into Sister's confidence so soon after taking up her post, and Caitlin knew it. She determined not to disappoint and to concentrate carefully on the possiblities for such an appointment. Meanwhile, there were the new patients to see.

The haemophiliac, Caitlin soon learned, was a taciturn young man who blamed himself for his admission to hospital. Caitlin chatted to him for about ten minutes, trying to reassure him, and in the end he settled down to a game of cards with one of the Professor's patients in the day-room.

Davy Selkirk was much easier to talk to, and very cheerful considering the gravity of his illness and his rather poor long-term prognosis. His progressive lymphatic disease had been controlled fairly successfully thus far, but the drugs used to keep it at bay had terrible and depressing side-effects.

Caitlin saw to the other two bedfast patients, checking their drips and fluid balance charts. They were both diabetics who had been de-stabilised over the holiday period by over-indulgence and with a cold, respectively. Both were recovering well.

Opening the side-room door, Caitlin met a pair of grinning, cheeky faces. Jamie and Robbie had transformed the room into a miniature aircraft hangar. Jamie Ferguson held a model out for her inspection.

'This one's a Fokker fighter. Isn't it fantastic?'

Caitlin was impressed. She saw that the thing was correct in every detail and a good two feet in wing span.

'Robbie's ma brought it in, and she's bringing in another the night, eh, Robbie? Isn't that right?'

Jamie was ecstatic. He had clearly never had toys like this made available to him before.

'She's bringing in one for me an' a',' Jamie continued. 'Fantastic!'

Robbie Rae studied the model aircraft in silence. He was obviously pleased, but a little embarrassed by his friend's eulogy.

'Well, Jamie. that's great. Now could you please leave Robbie to me for a couple of minutes? I've to give him his insulin now.'

' "I've to give him his insulin," ' mimicked Jamie. ' "So I have. I have, so I have." Okay, I'll leave you to it, Nurse O'Blarney.'

'And don't be so cheeky!' Caitlin told his retreating back.

He poked his head back into the room. 'Sorry!' he said, looking far from it.

She frowned hard at him, producing an extravagantly carefully closed door.

'So you've made a new friend, Robbie?'

'He's a' right. He's been helping me with this.'

'Is that the first one you've made? Or is it an old

hobby of yours?' she asked.

'Oh, I've made one or two,' Robbie said, 'but at home I've other things to do.' His voice trailed off as though he was uncertain whether or not to continue with what he was saying.

'What sort of things?' Caitlin encouraged softly.

'Oh, nothing much. Bird-watching, that sort of thing.' Robbie was offhanded. 'Skye's an island, see, and there's a' sorts up there. Seals an' a',' he added.

'That sounds nice, Robbie.'

'Aye, it's a' right,' agreed the boy.

Caitlin felt two sides of his character warring one with the other. There was the side which loved the simple pleasures of his country home, but he was half ashamed to admit that now. Since he had been in the city he had seen a different way of life. His glamorous mother's holiday home—Caitlin could imagine that, full of expensive bits and pieces that suggested rural life. And Jamie was forever talking about punk pop groups, football and motor-cycle racing. Robbie, she felt, was confused. His loyalties were split and he did not know where he belonged.

'I went to a lovely place yesterday, Robbie,' Caitlin told him.

'Oh? Where was that?' Robbie watched slightly nervously while she laid out on the bedtable a syringe, needle, sterile swabs and phials of insulin.

'A cove beside the sea at Cramond. You know the sea comes in to the Firth of Forth like this?' she drew the inlet between Edinburgh and Fife in the air between them. 'Well, you can get a bus from Princes Street and walk down to the edge of the water. You can get a ferry over the river. It's really super down there. I was enjoying it so much that I hardly noticed that it was getting dark, and then it began to show and . . .'

Caitlin stopped short and took a deep breath. 'There now, I'm talking far too much. I'm ready for the injection now. Are you? It's your left upper arm this time, I think.'

'That's right.' Robbie was too entranced by the cove to worry about his injection and submitted his slim arm to her without argument. 'And was the sea rough?' he asked.

'No,' said Caitlin, cleaning the skin with a sterile swab, 'it was cold and grey, like ruffled silver. And there were lots of seagulls. And a lovely bright moon came out, just for a minute. It peeped out between the clouds.'

She pinched up a fold of skin and administered the insulin at an angle of ninety degrees. She aimed to place the insulin in the tissues deep to the skin, yet avoid giving an intramuscular injection. This was the true meaning of 'subcutaneous', but it was too often badly done and either a blister resulted, or the insulin went into the muscles.

'You have to pull back the plunger like this before you inject,' she demonstrated with the used syringe. 'Just to make sure you're not in a blood vessel.'

'What if you are?' asked Robbie.

'Well, you have to come out and start again, because you don't want to give the insulin directly into your bloodstream. It'd get used up far too fast.'

'What's that place called, then?'

Caitlin refocused her mind in obedience to his mood.

'Cramond,' she told him, clearing away the kidney dish with used syringe, needle and insulin. 'It's not too far away—about twenty minutes on the bus. Perhaps when you're well your mother will take you there.' Caitlin meant Mrs Rae, but she didn't know how to say that.

'Mrs Rae's always going on about my jags an' a' that, an' how I'll be doing this when I get hame and that when I get hame. But I'm no' going to worry that much about the jags,' Robbie announced, to Caitlin's surprise.

She didn't have long to turn his words over. He soon made his meaning plain.

'My real mother says that if I tak' care I'll be right in no time . . .'

She sat down quickly on a chair next to him.

'Listen, Robbie,' she began, 'Mrs Rae is right. You'll have to do certain things every day if you want to stay fit and well. It's no good pretending you won't. If you take your injections and test your urine and so on, then you'll grow up fine, just like any other boy. You don't want to fall ill again, do you?'

'I'll no' fa' ill,' Robbie pouted. 'I'm no' an invalid.'

'I didn't say you were,' Caitlin replied. 'I said you'd have to take a bit of care of yourself.'

'I've got a job for you,' the boy returned, giving her a rebellious look.

Caitlin stood up. She had promised she would check insulin into a bottle of intravenous fluid with Nurse Adrian at two, and now it was just before.

'What's that?' she asked Robbie gently.

'Give this to Dr Sass for me?' He offered her a sealed envelope.

'Well, I don't see why not,' Caitlin answered. 'I'll be back in to see you later, Robbie.'

Outside, she read the childish, assertive handwriting on the envelope. She felt very unsettled indeed about Robbie Rae. She would speak to Sister about the conversation she had just had with him and discuss her fears, just as soon as she got the opportunity.

She tapped on the door of the doctors' room and got no reply, so she slipped in and placed the envelope on Dr English's desk.

'Dr Sassenach.' She glanced again at the addressee. She felt a pang. He was obviously just as available to his young patients now as he had been when she was

one. For a fleeting, irrational moment she envied
Robbie Rae.

Caitlin arrived at the bedside of her other diabetic
patient to find Nurse Adrian injecting insulin into the
drip bottle. The student nurse looked up implacably
at the approaching staff nurse, completed the injection,
then dropped the used syringe into a kidney dish on
the bedside locker. Reaching up, she scribbled ' +40
units U-100 Semilente, 2pm' on the label of the i.v.
bottle.

'Nurse Adrian, did Sister check the insulin in with
you?' asked Caitlin in surprise.

'No,' responded the girl flatly.

'Who did, then?'

'Nobody,' she answered.

'Why didn't you wait for me? I said I'd be back
here for two,' asked Caitlin.

'I thought you'd forgot.'

Caitlin checked the rate of flow of the drip and the
dose of insulin by the medicine chart, glanced at the
patient, who was dozing, then drew Nurse Adrian
away from the bedside.

In the comparative privacy of the nurses' station,
she faced her junior.

'You must never add drugs to a bottle of i.v. fluid
without checking them with another member of
staff—you know that. Even at your stage you should
check them with another nurse, preferably a senior
one. What were you thinking of?'

'Not much,' Nurse Adrian admitted sullenly.

A wave of irritation rose in Caitlin.

'What do you mean? How are we to work together
if you can't trust me to come when I say I will, or
wait for me?'

'It doesn't make much difference.'

'What do you mean?' Caitlin repeated.

'I've asked to be put on the change list, so I don't suppose I'll be here much longer.'

'But you sit your finals in six weeks or something, don't you? Why do you want to be moved just before you sit State?'

'Because this place is getting me down, that's why,' the student nurse responded insolently.

'Would you like to telephone Haematology for the Factor Eight for the haemophiliac, Nurse Adrian?' Caitlin responded quietly. 'It was on its way up ages ago, but it still hasn't appeared.'

She was furious. The student wandered off with a sidelong glance at her. What was going on with her? Caitlin was mystified as well as cross. The last thing anybody wanted was to be moved from one ward to another just before their State Registration examinations. It was crazy.

There was something up with Nurse Adrian. Perhaps she should mention this to Sister too. And then there was the business of the insulin not having been checked. That was definitely a reporting matter . . . What a day this was shaping into!

Caitlin checked empty containers, phials and bottles into the basket for pharmacy and ordered new supplies as needed. Part of her mind was still involved with the unpleasant duty of having to report Nurse Adrian to Sister Fairfield.

She hated to have to do it. She knew that Nurse Adrian was covering deeper things with her insubordination and carelessness. She was normally so painstakingly and religiously adherent to rules and regulations that it was hard to get her to relax into the atmosphere of the Unit sometimes when informality was to the benefit of the patients.

Something did not ring true at all. It was almost as though the younger girl had sought a confrontation with her, as if she had been challenging Caitlin's authority on purpose. Caitlin could not understand it.

Sister Fairfield, who had been at a meeting downstairs, reappeared at Caitlin's side looking cheerful and unperturbed. She had just heard the student nurse, Adrian, had put in for a change of ward and that SNO (allocation) was suggesting the Renal Unit for her.

The news had pleased Sister. She had not relished the idea of having to help the girl through her finals without the psychological support of a staffing post on the Unit waiting for her when she passed. It would be better all round for the girl to go soon and settle down somewhere else before her exams.

'Ah, staff, are you finished there?' she asked Caitlin. 'If so, would you like a cup of tea with me before I go off? I'm dying for one! These meetings are just interminable.'

Caitlin followed Sister to her room. Sister pulled off her scarlet cape and dropped into a chair. Caitlin filled the kettle and plugged it in.

'I wanted to speak to you about a couple of things . . .' she began.

'Not before I get a cup of tea inside me,' Sister warned.

Caitlin returned her smile and made the tea. She let it draw while she put biscuits on the table, then poured Sister and herself a cup each. Sister put hers directly to her lips and sipped the hot liquid with an expression of bliss.

'Okay,' she said, 'fire away!'

'Well, the first thing is about Robbie Rae,' Caitlin sat down next to Sister. 'I was speaking to him soon after I came on duty, and something he said worried me.'

'Oh?' Sister Fairfield raised her eyebrows. 'What might that be?'

'He just gave me the feeling that Miss Farrell has been making very light of his diagnosis. She has a lot of influence over him at present and I feel it's undermining our job of trying to teach him how to cope with his diabetes. It's a difficult situation with him, Sister.'

'And what about his adoptive mother? How has she been with him over this?'

'Well, she's quite different again,' Caitlin said carefully. 'She's much more down-to-earth and realistic about the whole thing, and she's been most responsive in the learning situation with the dietician and with us nursing staff. But Robbie seems to have taken completely against her. It's much easier for him to accept what Miss Farrell says and to turn his back on the truth.'

'It might be easier, but it's an awful lot more dangerous for him,' Sister interjected with concern.

'Exactly, Sister. That's what I mean . . .'

Caitlin did not have time to finish her sentence, for the door to Sister's office was violently opened and Dr English walked in. He marched up to Sister, apparently oblivious to all but the piece of paper he brandished in his hand.

'What's the meaning of this?' he asked ferociously.

Sister took the piece of paper and placed it face down on the coffee table.

'Would you like a cup of tea, Dr English? It's just made,' she invited pleasantly.

'I would most certainly not! And I'd like to know what the hell is going on here! What does this mean?' the physician hurled back at her.

Sister slowly and calmly picked up the piece of paper towards which he gestured, read it, then handed it to Caitlin.

A terrible silence reigned while she read:
'Dear Dr Sassenach,

I do not want to see Mrs Rae again. She is
not my mother. I have told Nurse O'Connell
too. She understands everything.

    Yours truely,

      Robbie.'

Caitlin looked up. She had never seen Jonathan
look like that. Fury, pain, goodness knew what struggled behind the mask of his face.

'So you understand everything, do you, Staff Nurse
O'Connell?' he articulated at last, his eyes smould-
ering. 'You understand . . . everything.' His voice fell
almost to a whisper, a strange inflection over the last
word.

Caitlin felt suddenly faint. She sat there, unable to
look away from his face, while he tortured her with
the accusation in his eyes.

'I think you *should* have a cup of tea,' Sister Fairfield
told him quietly. She poured a fresh cup, stood up
and put it down on her desk next to which he stood.

'Thank you,' he simmered, ignoring it.

'And I think you owe Staff Nurse an apology,'
Sister continued calmly. 'She's the last person to blame
for this—er—unfortunate affair . . .'

'She's the closest to him!' Dr English exploded.
'She's been responsible for his care ever since he was
admitted.'

'No,' Sister Fairfield asserted. '*I* have been responsible for his care, Dr English. *I* am Sister in Charge
of this Unit, and all your remarks and criticisms
regarding nursing care should be directed first to me.'
He glared at her, then turned and stormed towards
the door. There he turned round again and gave
Caitlin a look of complete disdain before slamming
the door behind him.

Sister Fairfield poured more tea for her staff nurse,

who looked thoroughly shaken. What had come over
Jonathan English she did not know lately, but he was
getting far too high-handed in his behaviour towards
her nursing staff.

She would give him a few minutes to cool his heels
and then go and tackle him about it. After all, what
was there to get so furious about? A childish whim.
And far more would be achieved through quiet, confident handling of the Rae child than with all this
medical hysteria . . .

'Drink your tea, lassie,' she told Caitlin. 'You've a
busy afternoon ahead of you. I'll have a word with
the good Sassenach on my way off, and I'll see you in
the morning.' She gave her staff nurse a conspiratorial
wink. 'The Sassenach with the sore head!' she remarked
jovially, 'that's him.' She picked up her cape and left.

The teacups were decorated with alpine flowers,
Caitlin noticed as she washed them up. She forced
herself to notice, especially while she emptied one still
full hot cup down the sink.

It was indescribable how his anger affected her. It
was as if her world stopped turning. Somehow she
had to make him see that she was not a child any
longer. Things could not go on like this between
them—not if they were to work together. And they
must be able to work together. At least while Robbie
Rae was their patient. After that perhaps she would
put in for a change of ward . . . something . . .
anything would be better than meeting Jonathan like
this and knowing he despised her.

'Mr Selkirk wants to speak to you,' Nurse Adrian
told her sulkily the moment she emerged from Sister's
office.

Nurse Adrian! She had completely forgotten Nurse
Adrian. So that unpleasant task still lay ahead of her.
Meanwhile, Caitlin was determined to try to improve
her relations with the student nurse. She invited her

to take her time over her tea as the Unit was not busy, and was rewarded by a sly, sulky look.

Mr Selkirk was sitting on his bed looking unhappy too. As she approached he was racked with a fit of chesty coughing.

'Oh, dear, Mr Selkirk! Can you get any of that up for me? We should get a specimen off to Bacteriology by the sound of it.'

Caitlin picked up the medicine chart from his bed table. It was completely blank. Obviously the doctors hadn't decided on any treatment yet. She would have to give the duty medical officer a ring and remind him to come up and write the patient up for some medication.

'It's no' the cough that'll carry me off, nurse!' Davy Selkirk smiled painfully, 'It's the pain in my chest.' He pressed his hand over his right lung and grimaced. 'It's right here, nurse.'

Pneumonia was just about the last thing that Davy Selkirk needed. Very often it was a urinary tract or a respiratory tract infection that did prove fatal for patients such as he.

'I think you should get back into bed, Mr Selkirk, and I'll put your pillows up high so that you can sit right up. Try to cough up that stuff on your chest and drink plenty of fluids. I'll get Nurse to bring you some fresh water. Have you got some squash in your locker?' Caitlin retrieved some orange juice and put it within reach on the locker top. She also put the bedrest up before screening the bed, and leaving him propped up comfortably in it.

Angus Dougan said he'd be up straight away, and he was as good as his word. He examined Mr Selkirk, then wrote him up for a broad-spectrum antibiotic to begin immediately pending the results of sensitivity tests on the specimen of sputum Caitlin had sent to Bacteriology.'

'And Staff O'Connell . . .' Dr Dougan began.

'Staff, Mrs Neil's drip's run through,' Nurse Adrian announced suddenly at Caitlin's elbow.

She excused herself from the doctor, saying she'd be back in a second, and rushed off to help putting up a new bottle of i.v. fluid on the drip.

Nurse Adrian maintained a sour distance, no matter how pleasant Caitlin tried to be with her during this operation and in spite of the fact that Caitlin withheld any criticism of the student in connection with it.

When she got back down the ward again, Dr Dougan was gone. In addition to all this, Dr English's words had settled in her soul like stones, and she was unable to feel enthusiastic when the clinical nurse specialist from the Renal Unit turned up. She much regretted this.

By nine o' clock she was exhausted. She sent Nurse Adrian off before giving the report to the night staff, then popped her head round Robbie's door to say goodnight. Nobody at all had visited him this evening. He had probably told Mrs Rae not to come and there had been no sign of Penelope Farrell. Caitlin felt defeated.

She was waiting for the lift when some instinct took her hand up to her breast pocket. The ward keys were still pinned inside it. Stupid! How easy it was to go off with the keys to the dangerous drugs cupboard, everything! She slipped back into the Unit and gave them to the night nurse in charge.

Dr Dougan caught her on her way out again.

'Hey, Caitlin, I wanted to ask you earlier. I see from the off duty sheet that you're off on Sunday. So am I. Shall we take the day out somewhere?'

Caitlin hesitated. She was so tired she couldn't think straight.

'Okay,' she said, 'I think that'd be all right, Dr Dougan.'

'Angus!' he said, obviously delighted. 'I'll pick you up around ten,' he added. 'See you then, then, if not before.'

Caitlin hesitated again before making for the lift again. What day was it today? She struggled with dates that belonged to another world. Tomorrow was Saturday, she decided at last. So she had plenty of time to change her mind about Angus's invitation. And that was about as far as she was capable of processing it tonight.

CHAPTER FIVE

CAITLIN was in charge next morning too, Sister's day off. She got in to the Unit early, praying for a quiet shift. Certainly, everything felt much calmer than it had last evening when she had left.

Both drips were down and Davy Selkirk had had a reasonably good night, having begun to respond to the thousands of milligrams of intramuscular Crystapen given him since six o'clock yesterday evening. Antibiotics had certainly revolutionised medicine, Caitlin reflected, just as the arrival on the scene of injectable animal insulins in 1921 had reversed the fate of diabetics the world over.

'And Robbie Rae had a restful night,' continued the night nurse who was giving the report. 'His treatment and rehabilitation continue as prescribed. He has requested not to see his adoptive mother, Mrs Margot Rae, and Dr English has advised her of this fact. Mrs Rae will be staying with her sister in Portobello for the duration of Robbie's admission. Her address and telephone number are here in the Kardex, and she's to be advised of any change in his condition.'

The night nurse paused.

'Oh, and wee Jamie excelled himsel' last night. Nurse Laing caught him creeping down the ward with his pockets full of grapes, biscuits and goodness knows all what.' She grinned at Caitlin. 'He was away for a midnight feast with his friend Robbie, it seemed.

'We gave him a good telling off, but being Jamie he had to have a full lecture on diabetes to satisfy him. He knew Robbie couldn't take chocolate and so forth, but he couldn't understand why he couldn't have biscuits all through the night!'

It was a full-time job trying to protect a newly-diagnosed diabetic from his friends and relatives, it seemed. Caitlin made a mental note to dissuade Robbie from fraternising too closely with Davy Selkirk too.

A mild upper respiratory tract infection or cold would be enough to destabilise Robbie's diabetes at this stage. The balance between insulin intake and bodily function and energy requirements was extremely delicate, and fighting a cold could tip the scales to his detriment.

She tried to concentrate on Robbie's physical needs in order to distract herself from his emotional ones, but she could never do so for long. She did not feel her preoccupation was misplaced. She did, however, feel unhappy at her basic lack of trust in the boy's natural mother.

She had constantly to remind herself to be fair to Penelope Farrell; to give her the benefit of the doubt. But somehow she could not convince herself that the woman had her son's best interests at heart. It was an unpleasant feeling.

'Nurse Adrian, would you take care of the Professor's patients again today?' she asked her colleague. It seemed the least she could do: to give the girl some continuity of responsibility for the same patients. It set Caitlin's mind at rest that she was doing all she could to make the student's lot easier. Anyway, there was a part-time staff nurse on too, so Caitlin had plenty of staff.

And Saturday was the one day of the week which seemed to permeate the walls of the hospital. Staff and patients seemed more relaxed, and the weekend atmosphere, without the bustle of operating theatre lists and outpatient department queues, was invariably casual and pleasant.

Caitlin got through the morning work quickly and without incident. The Unit was an easy one to run: the certain stamp of a good Sister in charge. Nurse Adrian worked methodically and thoroughly, avoiding Caitlin and addressing her queries instead to the part-time staff nurse.

After lunch, Caitlin encouraged the iller of the patients to take a nap. Saturday visiting hour was always busier than any other day of the week, and visitors, though they were so welcome, tired ill patients terribly.

Robbie refused to take a rest. He and Jamie were busy with a new model aircraft kit, which at least kept Robbie in his own room and out of range of Mr Selkirk's cough.

'It's great, eh?' Jamie prompted her the moment she appeared.

'Super. What is it?'

'A Harrier jump jet. Vertical take-off.' Robbie demonstrated with a flat hand rising straight up from the bedtable and an incredible sound-effect generated Caitlin knew not how.

'Very impressive,' she said.

'We'll have to paint it after,' Jamie told her. 'You can get wee pots of paint. Robbie's ma's bringing them in, eh, Robbie?'

'That's nice,' commented Caitlin noncommittally. 'So you two are just going to carry on all day without a rest, are you?'

'It's only old fogies needs rests,' Jamie informed her, 'Nurse O'Blarney Stone.'

'Oh? Is that so?' she countered. 'And that's how you got back on your feet, was it?'

Jamie eyed her mischievously.

'That's so,' he mimicked in Irish brogue.

Caitlin aimed a blow above his right ear which he expertly ducked.

But she left them to it and went to see Davy Selkirk. His four-hourly observations had been increased to hourly. He was pyrexial; the last temperature she had recorded was a hundred and two, and his coughing had subsided—a dangerous sign. A physiotherapist was busy with him, pummelling his chest in an effort to loosen the secretions which were gathering in his right lung.

Caitlin interrupted the physio to take his temperature, which was the same, but left pulse and respirations until he was more at peace. Mr Selkirk was as good-natured as ever, submitting to his treatment with amazing humour. Something made Caitlin very uneasy about him, nevertheless, and she hoped a doctor would appear to see him soon.

She was hardly back at the nurses' station before her hope was answered. Dr English passed her by without a word, wandered down the ward and screened the bed she had just left. A couple of minutes later the physio emerged, leaving the physician alone with her patient.

She shook her head at Caitlin.

'That's a pneumonia all right,' she said, 'I couldn't shift the consolidation in that right lower lobe at all. I'll be up tomorrow morning again, and I'll try postural drainage.'

'Poor Mr Selkirk,' murmured Caitlin. She sat down with his nursing notes and wrote them up to date. She wondered how many of these infections he had weathered before. She'd look at his medical notes, she promised herself, when Dr English had gone. She knew that Davy Selkirk had been lucky to reach adulthood, but somehow that thought did not comfort her.

The Unit physician dropped Davy's medicine chart down over the edge of the glass partition around the nurses' station so that it fell in front of Caitlin.

'Start this right away,' he said curtly. 'And come
and see me in my office as soon as possible after that.'

Caitlin swallowed her pride. He was being rude and
officious with her. Why? Her spirit rebelled against
him, and only the sense that Jonathan English
somehow could not help himself prevented her from
giving him a short answer. Still, she frowned at him
and said nothing.

He marched off. She picked up the medicine chart
and saw that Mr Selkirk had been started on oral
prednisolone. She unlocked the medicine cupboard
and put the tablets into a medicine cup, along with
the initial dose of a broncho-dilator and some potassium which had also been prescribed.

A few minutes later, having told the other nurses
where she was, Caitlin tapped on the doctors' room
door.

'Come in.'

She did so, closing the door quietly behind her. She
felt surprisingly calm. Being in charge always made
her feel calm, a result of her natural inclination for
taking responsibility.

Dr English came straight to the point.

'I want to speak to you about the Rae boy,' he
said.

Caitlin suddenly saw clearly that the physician was
taking advantage of Sister's day off.

'What about him, Dr English?'

'I think you should confine yourself to nursing him
and leave his private life alone.'

She did not answer. She met his level stare without
flinching.

'Do you understand me?' he asked.

'No, I do not understand you,' she replied distinctly.

A flush rose to Dr English's face so that he suddenly
looked very young again. It threw Caitlin off balance
for a moment and she clenched, then unclenched her

fists in nervous anticipation of what was to come.

'What do you mean?' His challenge was in his eyes.

She paused and took a deep breath.

'Dr English,' she said with emphasis, 'stop speaking to me as though I were a stranger to you.' She could take advantage of Sister's absence too, if that was the game he wanted to play. 'You know very well why I don't understand. It was you yourself who taught me the importance of emotional and family factors in the treatment and care of the newly-diagnosed diabetic.'

Dr English blanched.

'I do not want to be reminded of . . . all that,' he said, breathless with fury. 'I didn't ask you to speak back to me in that fashion. Who do you think you are?'

'I'm the staff nurse in charge of this Unit, at the moment,' Caitlin replied quietly, 'and I know I have absolutely nothing about which to apologise to you over my care of Robbie Rae.'

Dr English glared at her in total silence.

Externally she knew that she seemed to be in perfect control, but inside she was shaking. In his eyes was something which she could not grasp. It was as if he was trying either to tell her something or to hide it from her. She willed him to tell her what was going on in him. But that was not to be.

'It's often very difficult for . . . to distance oneself professionally from certain patients . . .' He paused significantly, 'especially when one is—er—at the outset of one's career. You're inexperienced as yet, Staff Nurse O'Connell. It's very easy to—er—identify too closely with a certain patient who . . .'

' . . . has diabetes too. Just like me!' Caitlin finished for him. She was livid at his pompous speech, furious at his condescension.

'You can go now, Staff Nurse,' he said.

She threw him a glance which she hoped contained

all her feelings. His dark eyes had darkened even farther and in spite of her anger, his face, his demeanour were agony to her.

'Thank you. Sir,' she added bitterly.

The door closed behind her, she closed her eyes for an instant, leaning against it. She made her way to the cloakroom to compose herself. Once there, staring at her own pale face in the mirror, she worked hard to transform her anguish back into pure anger.

He was impossible! What was he trying to do to her? He was completely unreasonable! His behaviour towards her was outlandish!

She felt better, comforting herself with the knowledge that it was he himself who had provoked her angry words to him. A sense of righteous indignation powered her through the rest of her shift, and she was glad she did not see him again.

Off duty, her mood persisted. The January Sales had begun and Princes Street was full of shoppers. In Marks & Spencers women searched remorselessly for bargains, and Caitlin soon abandoned her proposed purchase of tights and underwear.

Back outside the north-east wind tore through her anorak and chilled her to the bone. At first she thought that both hospitals and department stores were overheated, but then she decided she really did need a good coat.

She wandered down the Street, window-shopping, until a tap on her shoulder brought her face to face with Marian Forfar.

'Hello! How are you?' Marian looked pleased to see her. 'I was just thinking I needed someone to whom to confess I'd skipped lectures this afternoon so that I could enjoy it,' she said. 'Also, I'm rotten at shopping on my own.'

'So am I,' admitted Caitlin. 'I always try on every-thing and come away with nothing.'

'What are you looking for?'

'A fur coat, but . . .'

'A fur coat? Fantastic! There's a wee furriers just next to Forsythes. This way!'

It was useless for Caitlin to remonstrate. All her protestations about the suitability of such a garment, price, general indecision—all blew away on the cold north-east wind. Marian had appropriated the purchase of a fur coat, and that was that.

'It's beautiful, modom; a beautiful fit,' admired the shop lady, a blue-rinsed personage approaching the end of a long and successful career in fur coat selling, considered Caitlin. 'And it's no' dear—fifty per cent off that model. It's a discontinued line, you see.'

Caitlin was mesmerised by the refinement of the gracious Edinburgh accent, but somewhat nervous of Marian's obviously barely suppressed mirth.

'I have to say it's lovely on you, modom.'

Marian looked quickly away, and Caitlin looked obediently at herself in the full-length mirror. Actually, the coat did look super. It was a light-coloured 'fun fur' and it certainly was not expensive at a hundred pounds. She stared guiltily at herself. She knew her aunt had given her the money as a farewell present for exactly this purpose, but now that it came to spending such a huge sum on herself she just couldn't do it.

'We'll have it. Won't you, Caitlin?' Marian prompted her, back in on the act again in earnest.

'Very well, then . . . yes,' Caitlin agreed.

She wrote the cheque. It was done. The coat remained on her back, solid warm protection from the worst of Scottish winters, and her anorak was packed politely into a posh plastic carrier bag for her to take away.

She wondered ruefully if her life would ever quite match up to the wearing of a fur coat. But the train of thought only led back to Jonathan, yet again.

'And that's the first thing I'm treating myself to when—if I ever pass my finals,' said Marian with satisfaction.

Caitlin was touched by her capability for pleasure at someone else's purchase.

'Would you like a cup of coffee after all that decision-making?' she asked her.

'Great idea. I'll show you my favourite place.'

They went upstairs off George Street to a coffee house which was also a bookshop—a surprisingly compatible combination, Caitlin found. The atmosphere was unhurried and the coffee freshly made. She brought two cups and a couple of homemade cakes to the table Marian had found .

'Those are for you,' she said. 'I've brought my own plain biscuit.' She sat down. 'I'm a diabetic,' she added matter-of-factly, 'boring, isn't it?'

Marian cocked her head sideways and gave her new friend an appraising look. 'You don't look too bad on it,' she commented at last. 'Thanks for the buns.'

Caitlin grinned briefly and slipped out of her coat.

'It really looks super on you,' Marian said.

'It's very cosy,' said Caitlin. 'I'll wear it tomorrow.'

The remark was out before she had even realised she had accepted Angus's invitation. And then she thought of Marian.

'And where are you off to tomorrow?'

Caitlin hesitated briefly.

'Oh, Marian, Angus Dougan asked me to go out with him tomorrow and I agreed. I do hope that's okay with you?'

Marian sampled her cake with equanimity.

'Whew! He's a fast worker, that one! Of course it's okay with me. Angus and I are just good friends . . .'

'Thank goodness for that,' Caitlin replied. 'I'd rather a friendship with you than a love affair with the gorgeous Dr Dougan, if there has to be a choice.'

'No danger of losing me,' promised Marian, 'but I wouldn't like to say the same of your virtue.'

'Thanks for the warning,' said Caitlin, 'but I'm used to protecting that . . .'

She hardly realised what she had implied before they both collapsed into fits of giggles.

'Not that they've been exactly clamouring at my door, you know,' she managed to say eventually, 'but it's my convent education. I'm not always sure if it's working for me or against me . . .'

'Oh, Caitlin!' giggled Marian.

Before Caitlin knew it, she was telling Marian all about her last date in Dublin. And then about her parents, her hospitalisation, her early boy-friends and her struggle to train.

'You think you had problems? You should try to become a doctor as a mere member of the fair sex,' Marian replied with gall. 'Sex discrimination isn't in it, and they're as charming as they can possibly be with it. "They're pretty young things", I heard one hoary old professor tell a houseman one day of me, "but every one of 'em that gets a job takes it away from one of us, y'know". Can you believe that?'

'It's hard to believe,' Caitlin responded. 'Is it really that bad?'

'Worse,' the other girl asserted. 'But just you wait until it's me who's sitting on one of those selection panels! They'd better watch out they're wearing matching socks that day!'

Remembering this conversation much later, lying in her bath, Caitlin realised how far she had taken Marian into her confidence. It was against her reserved nature to have done so, but she was so glad of a new friend. She needed one. Especially after today.

And there he was again. She got out of the bath suddenly and violently, making herself dizzy. Damn, damn him! she thought, towelling her back with furious energy. She couldn't recall the last time she'd lost her temper like this, and now she had ruined her bath . . .

Today she had challenged Jonathan English to put their relationship discreetly back on its old innocent footing. Why had he refused?

North of Stirling the snow had lain. It iced the mountains, turning them into perfect, fairyland peaks. There was very little traffic on the roads, and once they'd left the motorway Caitlin felt Angus relax into the drive.

'How lovely it is up here,' she said.

'I like it,' her companion agreed, 'though there are plenty who find it too bleak for their taste.'

'I like it because it's so wild and there aren't any people,' Caitlin replied.

'Is Ireland pretty too? I've never been there,' Dr Dougan remarked.

'Ireland's . . .' A procession of seasons paraded through her mind. She saw the vibrant gorse, the purple blackberries and the misty autumn of her childhood. 'It's very pretty,' she said.

'All you ever hear about Ireland is the bad news,' commented Angus.

'Yes,' Caitlin replied simply, 'that's true.'

How would she begin to tell him what Ireland was really like? Homesickness, she had discovered, struck at the strangest moments. Just now, sitting beside this man in his car, she felt as though she were sixteen again, uprooted from her home. It was not simply that the sweater she'd pulled on over her jeans this morning was one her mother had knitted for her then. It was not even that she longed to be back there. It was a poignant mixture of emotions too potent to be described.

And then just as suddenly as the mood had come, it was gone, and the glens between the mountains with their frosted trees and dashing burns filled her with new excitement.

They took the road into the Trossach hills north of Callender, a river accompanying them for some way before emptying itself into a slender roadside burn a couple of miles north.

'How do you like the Unit?' asked Angus, once more breaking a long silence between them.

Caitlin found it difficult to be reminded of work, but she told him politely that she'd liked it so far. 'Sister Fairfield is nice,' she added.

'Yes, Ginny's a doll,' Angus agreed. 'Shame about her and Sass.'

She flashed him a glance which he appeared not to notice.

'She's been daft about him for years—well, as long as he's been around, so I gather,' he continued. 'But Dr English has other things on his mind. Work mainly, I suspect. You don't get to be a consultant at thirty for nothing . . .'

'Thirty! He must be more than thirty!' Caitlin exclaimed in spite of herself.

He gave her an amused glance.

'Well, I'm sure he'd be flattered to hear you say that! No, seriously, he must be about thirty-seven now. He's waiting for the Prof's job. He's a bit of a high-flier, our Sassenach. Anyway, may I assume that you've not lost your head to him already? Two of you on the Unit would be too much. And anyway, don't we lowly SHOs get a look in with the staff nurses nowadays?'

Caitlin tried to avoid the painful recollection that Jonathan English had been an SHO when she had first met him.

'Perhaps he's waiting until his Professorship before he settles down,' she suggested lightly. But her voice sounded false to her.

'Aye,' Angus agreed uncertainly, 'maybe.'

He drove in silence for a while.

'But I don't think he's the marrying kind,' he added eventually. 'That's Ben More,' he pointed out.

Caitlin gazed at the towering, cloud-clad summit to her left. She might as well relinquish any lingering hopes so far as Dr English was concerned, she decided, here and now. Even if he had not changed so drastically he would by now have become inaccessible to her; as unconquerable as the highest Himalayan peak.

She looked at the young man beside her and tried to reorientate her thoughts and aspirations. She was still working on it when they came to the small hamlet of Killin, nestling in a wooded valley beneath Loch Tay.

They found a pub where Caitlin chose hot shepherd's pie from the hob. It was good to share lunch in front of a roaring log fire, talking about nothing in particular.

Outside again the temperature had dropped and ice was forming like transparent lace around the rocks beside the river bed. Caitlin and Angus walked slowly up the road towards the waterfall and stood listening to its music. In early summer, swollen with the melted mountain snow, this was a torrent, but now it fell in cold crystal sheets, tinkling against the rocks like chandeliers.

Caitlin could not recall the last time that she'd taken time out of routine like this, not for a whole day. Her days off were spent shopping or doing other mundane things. She had spent many during the last year simply studying for her finals. She had forgotten how she loved to walk in the country. The day seemed suddenly wonderful.

She turned the collar up so that the fur of her new coat caressed her cheeks and strode beside Angus as though she belonged there. She pushed away the feeling that flitted through her telling her that it wasn't so.

'This is my favourite place,' said Angus. 'I used to come here when I was a child with my parents in Perth.'

They took the footpath for Loch Tay and followed its winding, narrow way all the way to the shores of the great lake. The silver mirror of its surface shone, winter trees reflected in its shoreside surfaces.

The light was failing when they reached the car again a couple of hours later. Angus had put his arm around her on the path back. She felt close to him, the day had been so nice, and she got into the car with a little sigh of regret that it was over.

'Thank you for bringing me here, Angus,' she said.

'My pleasure,' he replied sincerely. 'I hope we can get back before the weather breaks—I don't want us to have any walking we didn't plan on.' He looked up at the dark sky. 'I think it's going to snow again.'

They set off back to Edinburgh beneath the leaden, laden skies, and Angus drove with his arm resting along the back of Caitlin's seat. She felt comfortable and pleasantly tired after her walk. She realised now that she had been distinctly nervous of this date. Her last one had ended in disaster, as she had told Marian yesterday. She had walked out on her escort in the middle of a dance.

Angus seemed another type of man. She could not understand Marian's warning. He had behaved perfectly charmingly towards her all day. And as always when a man was not being pushy, Caitlin felt her guard down.

'Why did you want to be a doctor, Angus?' she

asked conversationally.

'Gory fascination,' he replied.

'No, seriously,' she insisted.

'Oh, I dunno. Maybe I wanted to do something positive for this miserable human race. Or maybe I wanted a good job with plenty of prospects!' Angus laughed.

He was handsome, his strong white teeth enhancing the clean symmetry of his face when he laughed. His eyes were kindly and full of amusement. Suddenly, he looked like the perfect young medical practitioner: intelligent, reassuring and confident.

'The former,' Caitlin decided.

'Very probably.' Angus Dougan thought for a minute. 'And what about you? Why nursing? Why not an actress, an astronaut or a model? Not that I don't think you're a model nurse. I do. You are.'

'I had diabetes diagnosed when I was seventeen,' she said impetuously. 'I got inspired with hospitals then.'

'But not with doctors?'

Caitlin's heart lurched painfully. Her surprise must have showed in her face, although her deep confusion could not have done.

'I mean, you never thought of doing medicine?' Angus smiled.

'No,' she said quickly. 'No, I never wanted to be a doctor. It's too far away from the patient for me.'

He gave her a searching look, which made her blush.

'That's probably why you're such a super nurse,' he said. 'Anyway, you chose the right place to do it. Edinburgh's a fine place for medicine and nursing and always has been. Then there was the famous Irishman, Mr Burke . . .'

Caitlin was so relieved that the subject had changed that she forgot to worry about distasteful jokes about her countrymen.

'And what did he do?' she asked.

'Oh, he snatched bodies. They hanged him in 1829, I think it was.'

She made out the craggy form of Ben More on her right and shivered.

'Body-snatching?' she queried.

'Yes. He stole bodies from the graveyards and then sold them.'

'What's that got to do with medicine?' she asked nervously.

'He sold them to medical students!' Angus pronounced the words with mirthful relish. 'For dissection.'

'What a horrible story!' Caitlin shuddered.

'Yes, isn't it?' Angus replied with equanimity. 'There's a pub named after him and his crony, a Mr Hare. I'll take you there one of these days.'

'Thank you,' said Caitlin dubiously,' but I don't think I'd fancy a drink.'

She enjoyed the rest of the drive, listening to Angus talk about his student days of study, exams and parties. It seemed that one needed the capacity of a sponge to soak up medical facts for finals. And new findings were coming on to the syllabus all the time. She found she envied poor Marian less and less. Nursing seemed a far more fulfilling job emotionally than medicine could ever be.

The car drew up in front of a large building which faced on to the Firth of Forth at Queensferry, just outside Edinburgh.

'This is a nice inn,' Angus told her. 'I thought I'd show you it. It's a famous one.'

The wind was better, and Caitlin found tears in her eyes as she tried to gaze up into the cobwebbed girders of the huge railway bridge that spanned the Firth. She was standing almost directly underneath it. The bridge

lunged across the black water like a fallen Eiffel
Tower, its modern compatriot leaning gracefully beside
it bearing a road linking the Lothians with Fife.

Angus put an arm protectively around her shoulders.
'Impressive, eh?' he said.

'Amazing!' She watched a gull sweep across the
dark water and come to rest upon a rusty girder.

'Come on, it's cold out here.'

Angus pushed open the door of the pub, and Caitlin
was completely unprepared for what came next.

Jonathan English and Penelope Farrell sat in the
corner of the saloon bar, the only customers in it.
They were locked in passionate discussion, his eyes
searching hers.

Dr English suddenly became aware that they were
not alone, spun round and saw Caitlin and her
companion in the doorway. There was no mistaking
how he felt about it.

Caitlin turned and walked blindly out again,
brushing past Angus as she did so.

'Hey, where are you going?'

'I'm sorry,' she said outside, 'but I don't want to
go in there.'

'He won't eat you,' Angus teased. He had obviously
interpreted her reaction as girlish junior hospital nurse's
nerves. 'Even a consultant can enjoy a pint of heavy,
you know. Mind you, I don't think much of the
company he keeps. He certainly looks his age tonight!'

Angus was evidently vastly amused. Caitlin fought
her desire to tell him to shut up. She had known the
SHO just long enough to recognise in him that rare
breed, the male gossip, and she didn't fancy drawing
his attention to her own miserable state.

It seemed impossible to hold her head up in front
of Jonathan English since they'd met again. He was
obviously determined to treat her as the most junior
of junior nurses at work, and worse, one who got

Open your heart to love with 2 Best Seller Romances FREE

Can you resist the promise of wild, passionate romance...the shy glances, the stolen kisses, the laughter – and the tears? If, deep within your heart, you're a true romantic, then these are love stories for you. Stories that comprise a unique library of books from Mills & Boon – we call them Best Seller Romances. From the very first page you'll understand why these books have enthralled thousands of readers and now rank among our Best Sellers.

As your special introduction to our most popular library, we'll send you 2 Best Sellers and an exclusive Digital Quartz Clock FREE when you complete and return this card.

Now, if you decide to become a subscriber, you can receive four Best Seller Romances delivered directly to your door, every two months. If this sounds tempting, read on; because you'll also enjoy a whole range of special benefits that are exclusive to Mills & Boon. For example, a free bi-monthly newsletter packed with recipes, competitions, exclusive book offers and much more – plus extra bargain offers and big cash savings.

Remember, there's absolutely no obligation or commitment – you can cancel your subscription at any time. So don't delay any longer...complete, detach and post this card today. The romance of your dreams is beckoning – don't keep it waiting!

PLUS A QUARTZ CLOCK and a Mystery Gift FREE

FREE BOOKS CERTIFICATE

Dear Susan,

Your special Introductory Offer of 2 free books is too good to miss. I understand they are mine to keep with the Free Clock and mystery gift.

Please also reserve a Reader Service Subscription for me. If I decide to subscribe, I shall receive 4 new books every two months for £4.40 post and packing free. If I decide not to subscribe, I shall write to you within 10 days. The free books and gifts will be mine to keep in any case.

I understand that I may cancel or suspend my subscription at any time simply by writing to you. I am over 18 years of age.

6A7BB

Name _____
(BLOCK CAPITALS PLEASE)

Address _____

_____ Signature _____

_____ Postcode _____

Mills & Boon reserve the right to exercise discretion in granting membership. Offer expires 31st December 1987. You may be mailed with other offers as a result of this application. Valid in UK only, overseas please send for details.
Please note Readers in Southern Africa write to: Independent Book Services P.T.Y., Postbag X3010, Randburg, 2125 South Africa.

To Susan Welland
Mills & Boon Reader Service
FREE POST
P.O. Box 236
CROYDON
Surrey CR9 9EL

SEND NO MONEY NOW

emotionally involved to the detriment of her patients' care.

And now she had contrived to barge in on some sort of private meeting between him and Penelope Farrell and been rewarded with a look that would have sliced straight through hippopotamus hide, let alone through her own thin skin.

She tried hard to avoid the painful and obvious implications of the scene that she had just witnessed and concentrated instead upon her own predicament.

'I think I could do with a meal, Angus,' she said. 'Would you mind if we just went straight back into town?'

CHAPTER SIX

ANGUS hadn't minded. In fact, he'd seemed quite keen to get back to Edinburgh, and it wasn't until much later, after their Italian meal, that Caitlin began to realise why.

He invited himself into her room for coffee and planted himself firmly in her armchair. She declined his offer of his knee and curled up instead on the rug some way off.

She wished he would go. She badly needed time to think; her mind was in turmoil. Instead the SHO sat there looking plaintively at her, obviously hurt by the distance she'd put between them.

'Do you have . . . anyone back home, Caitlin?' he asked at last.

She considered her reply for a full minute, but in the end she couldn't lie.

'No, not really,' she admitted.

'I like you, Caitlin,' Angus said, encouraged, 'and I'd like to get to know you a lot better.'

She wished the floor would open and swallow him up. Or her. But not both of them together. Why, oh, why did he have to spoil a perfect day with this stupid . . . talk?

He edged off the armchair and joined her on the floor, and she searched desperately for words to say. A sudden knock on the door nearly scared her out of her wits, but then she was up and across the room like greased lightning.

'Marian!' she exclaimed, overjoyed at this timely interruption. 'Come in!'

'Hi!' said Angus, his dejection plainly written on his face.

Marian seemed instantly to assess the situation.

'Oh, Angus! Caitlin looks exhausted. What have you been doing to her?'

'Nothing!' he groaned ironically.

'Why on earth don't you go home and let her get to bed?'

Angus got up and put his jacket on resignedly, with only the smallest rueful glance at Marian for her helpful suggestion. He knew when he was beaten, it seemed.

'Thank you for a super day, Angus!' said Caitlin, now free to express her appreciation.

'Thank *you*,' he insisted ambiguously. At the door he kissed her lightly on the cheek. 'See you soon,' he said softly.

After he had gone the two girls gossiped happily for another hour. Marian said that the architecture student had finally asked her out after screwing up his courage for over a year, and how had Caitlin's day gone?

'Really, it was very nice,' said Caitlin. She told her friend all about Killin. 'But I was pretty pleased to see you just now!' she added.

'So I saw. Poor old Angus!'

'Well, I can't help it.'

'Didn't you enjoy his company today?'

'Yes. But not that much.'

'Poor old Angus,' Marian repeated. 'I think he's quite smitten with you, Caitlin.'

'Isn't he smitten with anything new that comes along?'

'Not quite this smitten,' replied Marian with amusement. 'Still, it's certainly a change for Angus to get a cool reception for once. And all's fair, they say, in love and war!'

*   *   *

Love and war, Caitlin reflected bitterly a couple of weeks later. They both seemed equally to describe her relations with Dr Jonathan English, FRCP Edin.

At least her New Year resolution was proving much easier to keep than she had at first thought it would be. That was about the most positive point she could make out in the whole affair. That, and the fact that he had taken annual leave, or something, so that she hadn't seen him for a while—since the incident at Queensferry, actually.

She pinned on her cap with mixed feelings. Each time she returned to the Unit after her days off she told herself she was prepared for anything the coming shift might bring, but today she felt distinctly unprepared.

So she was hardly surprised when the first thing it presented her with was Jonathan. He came out of Robbie's room at exactly the same moment she emerged from the cloakroom and gave her a searing look.

'Good afternoon,' she managed.

'Is it?' he returned.

She told herself firmly on the way to the nurses' station that it was none of her business what he had been doing with Penelope Farrell at Queensferry; it only concerned her that she retain some dignity under his abuse.

She dwelt again on the bitter thought that had possessed her after Marian had left that night: that from all she knew of the new Dr English, he and Penelope Farrell suited one another admirably.

But she was still trembling when she sat down for the report, and it did nothing for her self-confidence to note that Nurse Adrian was on late with her yet again.

Sister Fairfield gave Caitlin a smile of welcome,
then looked up with surprise at the tall figure of the
consultant, who had apparently followed her to the
station.

'Do sit down and join us, Dr English,' she invited.
'Staff Nurse O'Connell, nice days off, I hope?'

Caitlin struggled to make her voice sound normal.

'Super, thank you, Sister.'

'And I hope you had a pleasant holiday, Dr English?
What can I do for you?'

'I've stopped the Rae boy's insulin, stat,' he
announced shortly. 'I want all his urinalysis results on
my desk as soon as they're done and we'll see what
happens from here. I've just spoken to the boy and
I'll see his—er—mother this afternoon. It seems he's
gone into a honeymoon period . . .'

To Caitlin's horror Dr English glared straight at
her as he said these words. And she knew for absolute
certain that he was referring to her having been with
Angus Dougan last time they met. The blood rushed
to her face and she was forced to stare down at her
apron. She felt outraged and deeply embarrassed by
this public scene and completely powerless to do
anything about it.

'Staff O'Connell,' Sister addressed her, 'will you
ring Mrs Rae and explain what's happening? If you
could keep an eye on Robbie Rae this afternoon too,
especially about the time his insulin would have been
due. I assume you understand what Dr English is
referring to when he speaks of a "honeymoon period"?'

Briefly, Caitlin met the dark eyes of her adversary.
She found something that she took to be mild humour
there, and it took her aback. Once he had looked at
her like that—when he'd teased her for blushing as a
young girl in Dublin.

A stab of pain shot through Jonathan at the moment
when he looked at her. He remembered her colouring

when he'd teased her in the ward in Dublin. The memory made the glimpse he'd had of Caitlin with Angus Dougan even more acute. Angus Dougan! He was no match for her.

He composed his features and swallowed hard.

'Oh, I'm sure she does, Sister,' he persisted, in spite of himself. 'I should imagine she's quite an expert on the subject, eh, Staff Nurse O'Connell?'

Caitlin flushed again, this time with pure fury.

'Yes, Sister, you could say that,' she told Sister pointedly. 'I think I'm in a position to explain adequately to Mrs Rae what's happening with the boy.'

Sister Fairfield looked from her staff nurse to the physician and back again with puzzlement. She could not fathom what was going on between these two, but she did know from long years of hospital experience that chemical antagonisms could spring up between staff members for no apparent reason and that the intense atmosphere on a unit such as this one could transform such friction into fire very quickly.

'Fine, then,' she said. 'If there's nothing else, Dr English, I should like to get on with the report.'

Caitlin watched the consultant wander off down the Unit towards Mr Selkirk's bed. As her anger subsided, she found herself noting how tired Jonathan's step was, how bowed his shoulders. He had lost his old athletic vigour.

She had to drag her attention back to the report again and again. It was far easier to be angry with Jonathan English than to worry about him, wonder about him and try to understand his changed personality, she found.

Two hurdles had to be crossed before she could get down to work this afternoon. She decided to tackle the worst one first. She waited until the other nurses had dispersed after report, then she cornered Sister Fairfield.

'Sister, I meant to tell you ages ago, but we got distracted. Nurse Adrian put insulin into a bottle of i.v. fluid without checking it with another member of the nursing or medical staff the other week. I don't know what came over her. She's usually so meticulous about these things . . .'

'Very well, Staff, you don't have to feel you need to make excuses for the girl,' said Sister. 'You're quite right to report the matter, and I'll speak to Nurse Adrian.'

'She told me she's put in for a change of ward, Sister, and I couldn't understand it, so near to State.'

Sister Fairfield balanced the advantages of confiding in her new staff nurse and decided they were outweighed by the confidentiality she owed the junior nurse. It was a shame, but she didn't want the Irish girl to feel at all guilty or unhappy about her own post either. She would speak to Nurse Adrian about the misconduct over the insulin.

And she'd try to remember to speak to Claire Duncan, Sister on the Renal Unit, about the possibility of some counselling for the third-year student. She seemed to have taken the loss of a staffing opportunity on UYCS very hard indeed.

Sister sighed loudly. What with Nurse Adrian, and Jonathan behaving like a schoolboy, and prima donna pubescent patients—her private heaven of a medical unit was tending dangerously towards the hellish!

'And so it's just a matter of waiting to see what happens, Mrs Rae,' Caitlin concluded. Privately, she cursed the telephone. She had no real idea of the effect her words were having; the instrument was hopeless where feelings were concerned.

'And you say this might go on for a month or even a year? That he'll no' need ony treatment? That's awfully strange, nurse. And then the jags and everything will have to start up again? What a shame for the wee lad! We'll have to try our best to help him over it, won't we?'

'That's right, Mrs Rae. The main thing to remember is that this honeymoon period, as it's called, is not permanent and that it's just his body reacting to the insulin we've given him. It's as if it's been reminded of the job it should have been doing all along and so it produces insulin itself. But then it will forget again and the diabetes will reassert itself. It's just a matter of time, I'm afraid, before the symptoms reappear again.'

'That's very hard on him,' Margot Rae said in soft tones.

'It is, Mrs Rae, but we'll all try to make it as easy for him as possible. The doctor has been in to him this morning and explained everything, so we just have to hope he's understood properly and can take things in his stride.'

'Well, it's good of you to let me know everything that's happening, nurse,' said Mrs Rae after a short pause. 'I suppose he's no' asked for me yet? His mother'll have been in, I suppose?'

Caitlin swallowed the lump that had risen to her throat. It broke her heart to hear Mrs Rae's timid questions.

'No, he hasn't asked to see you yet, Mrs Rae,' she said gently, 'but I'm sure he will one day. And yes, Miss Farrell has been in most days. Robbie has found a friend of his own age on the Unit, and he's quite settled in.'

'Oh well, that's super, nurse. I'll say cheerio then—and give him my love, would you?'

Caitlin put down the receiver, clenching her right hand in her habitual way when she was stressed. Something told her that Penelope Farrell would not react in the same sensible, foresighted way to news of Robbie's remission. Why, oh, why had he refused to see his adoptive mother when she could help him so much?

The thought was still circulating in her head when she found her young patient in the day-room. He and Jamie had graduated from model aeroplanes to rock music and were taking turns listening to a portable tape recorder through headphones. Currently, it was Robbie who was listening, a faraway look in his eyes.

'It's a fantastic sound!' Jamie told Caitlin.

'I suppose Robbie's mother brought it in for him?'

She could not help her voice sounding a trifle jaded, but such subtleties were lost on Jamie.

'Aye. An' she's bringing in some more tapes the night,' he enthused. 'What music do you like, O'Blarney?'

Caitlin considered.

'Stevie Wonder's good,' she said eventually. 'And Paul McCartney.'

'Paul McCartney!' scoffed Jamie. 'He's *ancient*! You're as bad as Dr Sass; he likes Elton John and Mick Jagger. Ever heard of they old fogies?'

Caitlin grinned.

'I like them too,' she said.

'Pooh!' retorted Jamie in disdain. 'You're a right pair, you are!'

She turned this comment over rather sorrowfully in her mind.

She eventually managed to extract Robbie from his headphones and from the day-room. He was reluctant to accompany her and only sulkily agreed to test his own urine while she watched to make sure he did it right.

'I don't see much point in doing this any more,' he grumbled, adding a Clinitest tablet to the test-tube.

'What do you mean?' Caitlin questioned sharply. It

was exactly the sort of thing she dreaded hearing from him.

'Dr Sass says I'm getting better. He's stopped my insulin. Look on the chart,' Robbie replied.

'Oh, Robbie, it's no good talking like that,' she said, charting the result of his urinalysis and keeping the chart to put in the doctors' room.

He made for the door.

'Hey, wait a moment!' she said, catching him by the arm. 'Listen, I want to speak to you for a minute.'

He sat down grudgingly, his eyes averted from her.

'Dr Sass didn't say you were getting better, Robbie,' she began gently, 'not completely better.' She went through the explanation she had just given to the boy's adoptive mother. 'And so, you see, although it seems as though you're better, you're not really, and it's just your body pretending that it wasn't unwell at all. But then it'll get lazy again and you'll need to get insulin again.'

'Stupid!' Robbie gave her an aggressive stare. 'It's just stupid,' he repeated angrily.

'Yes,' Caitlin agreed, 'it's a darn stupid business, this diabetes.'

He glared back at her and for a crazy instant she was reminded of the consultant who had given her just such a look not so very long before.

'Anyway, I'm going now,' the boy said.

Caitlin was left to tidy up and to wonder what sort of joke this was of Nature's. A 'honeymoon period' indeed! Robbie Rae needed this remission just about as badly as a hole in the head. She was full of sympathetic annoyance. It was ridiculous for so young a person to have to try to cope with so fickle a disease.

'Been counselling the patient, have you, Staff Nurse O'Connell?' Dr English's smile was a travesty. 'I just had a few words with him while we were testing his urine.' Caitlin was taken completely unawares.

The consultant closed the door behind him and the side-room instantly transformed itself into a torture chamber for her. She stood there trembling, thinking he must be able to hear her heart.

Dr English stared at her, daring her with his eyes to speak, to move, to respond in any way, and when he saw that she did not dare to do any of these things he managed to control his own desire to do so.

Instead he thought about the boy. It was ridiculous to be jealous of a child's affection. What was the matter with him? They didn't teach you this at medical school. They didn't tell you that you had emotions as well as a scientific mind. Or how hard to school emotions were.

He knew he owed it to Robbie to be kind to Caitlin O'Connell. He owed it to himself. But women . . . the child . . . it was more than a man could stand. The vision of the Farrell woman's face while he'd pleaded with her at South Queensferry haunted him. She would never let the child go. Not now.

And if that was what Robbie wanted too, what could he do? She was not fit to look after the boy alone.

Caitlin flinched as the consultant shrugged his shoulders aggressively at her. She could not imagine what was going on in his mind or why he should be so furious with her for her care of Robbie. She couldn't do anything right for him. She didn't want another confrontation with Dr English. She wished he'd excuse her, ignore her—anything would be better than this.

He was wondering whether he would have to bring himself to marry the Farrell woman after all . . . after all, when Caitlin pushed Robbie's urinalysis results chart into his hand.

'I'm not Robbie's counsellor, Dr English,' she said softly and with care. 'I'm only his nurse.'

Only, thought Jonathan, unable to tear his eyes away from her face. Only!

'You underestimate yourself,' he muttered, 'as I think I told you once before.'

She shuddered, trying to keep calm.

'I . . .' she began.

But their fingers were still touching as the chart transferred hands and she was unable to focus on anything but the warm fingers that touched her own.

'Thanks . . . Staff Nurse,' he said.

They made as if to open the door simultaneously and each stopped, hesitated and then stifled an embarrassed laugh. Then the consultant took the new opportunity she offered him and marched briskly out ahead of her.

Charming! thought Caitlin, smoothing her apron. But she was glad for a chance to savour that ridiculous, intimate moment that they had just shared before she had to face the outside world once more.

Caitlin had expected Sister to speak to the girl about the insulin incident; she had not been prepared for the aftermath.

Everything she asked Nurse Adrian to do, however sweetly and politely, was carried out with an air of resentment and reproachful silence intervened.

At about four-thirty she had to ask Angus to come up and see Mr Selkirk, who was running a fever again. She settled the patient as best she could, gave him a sip of water through a straw, then went to let the visitors in.

Penelope Farrell arrived on the Unit first, resplendent in furs as usual. She greeted Caitlin with enthusiasm and swept into Robbie's room on the dot of half past four. Jonathan, Caitlin noted, followed her in. It was as if he'd been waiting for her.

Angus appeared a couple of minutes later, and Caitlin was able to speak to him before he went to Mr Selkirk's bedside. She was glad the latter had no visitors; he looked awful. She screened the bed and smiled encouragingly at him.

'Only VIP visitors for you today, Davy,' she said, glancing up as Angus arrived.

'He never brings me grapes, nurse,' Mr Selkirk returned with a wry grin.

'Next time, Mr Selkirk,' promised Dr Dougan. He began to undo the top of the patient's pyjama jacket very gently. 'Now then, let's have a listen to this chest, shall we?'

The next morning Davy Selkirk was worse. As if to comfort Caitlin, Robbie Rae was as bright as a button. He seemed to be coping perfectly well without extraneous insulin and his diabetes seemed magically to have disappeared.

Caitlin allowed her concern for Mr Selkirk to dominate her mind. She hated it when screens stayed around a bed all day. She always had, ever since her training days. The other patients always knew that something was badly amiss and went up and down the ward on tiptoe, whispering. It was dreadful for them if something happened to one of their number: the comrades of the ward dinner table and day-room.

A conspiracy of silence prevailed, as usual; the nurses said nothing to the other patients and they didn't ask for information from the nurses—as if afraid to hear the worst.

Sister Fairfield went so far as to mention all this to Caitlin at coffee time. But as she said then, what could you do, short of issuing bulletins on ill patients to the others? As long as open wards persisted, so would the problem.

The worst of it was, it was demoralising for every-body, and the artificial bonhomie generated to disguise it was downright depressing. No amount of bonhomie could help Davy Selkirk where modern medicine had failed. The most it could do was to make that failure bearable—in the most unbearable way.

Caitlin was glad when Sister asked her to take the Professor's ward round. It would involve her in 'the other side's' patients for a change, and she felt it was about time they shared her attention. Professor Carstairs had a happy knack of admitting patients who got better the instant they set foot in the Unit.

Still, she was surprised to find the round stopping outside Robbie Rae's room, even if he did seem to qualify for this category. She decided that Dr English must have felt that two days was too long between examinations of 'the Rae boy' in his current delicate situation and had asked the Professor to see him on his rounds too.

Professor Carstairs stepped into the side room slightly ahead of his entourage. Caitlin knew only Dr Dougan of the three doctors on the round. In addition there were two medical students, a girl and a man.

Robbie was sitting obediently beside his bed, but Caitlin's expert eye detected rebellion in the set of his shoulders.

'Now, laddie, how are we today?'

'A'right.'

Robbie was not wasting words today, not even to impress the Professor.

'Now, what have we here? Notes, please, Staff Nurse . . . O'Connor?'

Robbie smirked and Caitlin lifted her eyebrows at him challengingly.

'O'Connell, Professor,' she said.

'As in Street?'

'Yes, sir,' smiled Caitlin, as much at the recollection

of her beloved Dublin as at the Professor.

'Lovely place, Dublin. Many a pleasant memory I've got,' he said. He paused nostalgically. 'Used to examine there years ago,' he said, 'the old Fellowship exams, you know. Now,' he returned his attention to the notes in front of him, 'a newly diagnosed diabetic who suddenly stops needing his insulin. What's all this about? Can you tell us, Miss Green?'

The Professor smiled benignly at the girl medical student, who coughed nervously. Watching the other medic exchange amused glances with his qualified colleagues, Caitlin once more pitied Marian her choice of career.

'Um . . . I think it's . . .' the girl began.

Caitlin willed her to recall the syndrome, saying it over and over in her own mind. Suddenly the girl's face flooded with relief.

'It's the "honeymoon period",' she said triumphantly, and the signs, symptoms and prognosis tripped off her tongue with textbook ease.

Caitlin kept her eyes modestly averted from the frank astonishment in the faces of her medical colleagues. But she did not have long to ruminate upon the rights and wrongs of sex discrimination in medicine, or to commit the scene faithfully to memory for relay to Marian.

'Quite so, Miss Green. I couldn't have put it better myself. And a weekend at home would do us the world of good, eh, young fellow?' Professor Carstairs beamed over the tops of his half-moon glasses at Robbie.

Robbie jumped, then looked to Caitlin for confirmation of the Professor's words. She avoided his eyes, waiting to hear more herself, herself completely taken by surprise.

'Can we arrange that, then, Staff Nurse? A weekend at home to see how we manage without a wardful of doctors and nurses to look after us, eh?'

He smiled briefly at Robbie once more, and was gone.

'I'll be back in to see you as soon as the ward round's over, Robbie,' Caitlin hissed as she passed him on her way out.

But Robbie was in another world. His face was flushed and his eyes unnaturally bright.

'See?' he breathed at her. 'I *told* you I was better!'

She closed her eyes in momentary exasperation.

'I'll see you in a second,' she repeated.

She knew it would take all the skill she possessed to introduce a note of reason into the highly-charged state left behind in the Professor's wake.

It did. Robbie's euphoria over the impending weekend was matched only by his mother's. Over the next few days, Penelope Farrell drove all the staff half crazy with her pretentious requests to see the Professor and the general impression she tried to create of being a private patient—or, at least, of Robbie being one.

She was completely carried away by the prospect of the weekend, as if the Professor's trust in her was evidence incarnate of her perfection as a mother.

Meantime, Caitlin coped with discharges, admissions, Nurse Adrian, staff meetings, Jamie's jealousy and a severe deterioration in the condition of Davy Selkirk.

By the time Friday lunchtime arrived she was glad to find herself in the canteen queue next to Angus. He was his usual off-duty stalwart, friendly, slightly bantering self, and just what Caitlin needed.

'Fancy a picture tonight, Caitlin?' he asked without ceremony as they carried their trays to an empty table. 'It's a while since I've seen a decent film, and the one on at the Caley's been well reviewed.'

'I'd love it, Angus,' Caitlin agreed.

Back on the Unit she gritted her teeth and waited

for her shift to end. But as usual when she was in this rare mood, there was plenty in store for her yet.

In the side-room she began packing Robbie's tooth-brush, face-cloth and soap into his toilet-bag in preparation for the weekend. Something worried at the back of her mind as she did so, some nagging anxiety that she had tried to push away a hundred times since the Professor's fateful ward-round.

She wondered where Jonathan was; she had not seen him around for a couple of days. She zipped up the toilet-bag and pushed it into the open holdall on the bed. She hoped Robbie would be all right.

'I'm surprised he's not taking you with him.'

She spun round to meet Jonathan English's serene, sarcastic stare. In her mind, still fresh, was the warning that the physician had delivered to Robbie and which Robbie had reported to her yesterday: that he was not to be left alone or to lock himself in anywhere in case he took a 'turn' and could not be found.

All the tension of the past few days released itself in her.

'I wish he could!' she declared.

She defied him to accuse her of over-involvement. She defied him with her eyes to answer her at all.

To her surprise, he didn't.

He quietly turned and left the room, only asking softly as he left where 'the Rae boy' was.

Caitlin followed him down to the day-room when she had finished packing a few moments later. Robbie was on his own again, restlessly waiting for Miss Farrell to appear, his cheeks flushed with excitement.

'Guess what!' he greeted Caitlin, his eyes shining. 'Dr Sass's got the weekend off too and he's to give me and Mother a lift to her house. Isn't that fantastic?'

'It's very kind of him,' Caitlin replied, her heart thumping painfully.

Barely ten minutes later she was treated to the sight

of Penelope Farrell with her arm around Robbie's
shoulders, smiling graciously meanwhile into the eyes
of an elegantly-suited Jonathan English. Caitlin tried
not to feel that he looked somehow defenceless without
his white coat, or to make too much of a certain
strain about his expression. He had probably been
working too hard and was looking forward to his
weekend off.

She bade Robbie farewell and answered Miss
Farrell's final, superficial queries about his care. And
at last they were all three gone, leaving only a pain in
Caitlin which she could not name. It was no good
denying how beautiful Miss Farrell was, after all. And
there was no point trying to hide from the fact that
Jonathan found her fascinating. What else would
prompt him to turn himself into her chauffeur?

She concentrated her attention from now on on Mr
Selkirk, whose temperature had risen to a hundred
and four. She spent the next hour tepid-sponging him,
to no effect. Angus came down just before she went
off, examined Davy and wrote him up for more
medicament, but Caitlin could tell from his face that
they were only palliative. Angus no longer hoped to
cure him.

'I can't help feeling miserable about him, Angus,'
she said as they waited to buy tickets. 'He's such a
nice man, and he never complains.'

'Perhaps he feels lucky to have survived so long,'
Angus suggested.

'Still,' she said softly, 'still, poor man.'

'You shouldn't take your work off duty with you,'
he rebuked her, 'And if you must do so, why not the
success stories? What about your wee friend Robbie
Rae? He's got a long and healthy life ahead of him,
thanks to an early diagnosis, excellent nursing
care . . .' he squeezed her hand . . . 'and so on.'

'Yes, Robbie's all right,' Caitlin replied. She was

thinking, Robbie's all right, it's his mother who worries me. But she decided that this was definitely too unethical to share with the SHO.

He paid for two tickets and they went into the foyer. Caitlin loved going to the cinema. It retained for her the thrill of teenage excursions to the local picture house—a real treat. She sat down beside Angus in the darkened auditorium.

'It's just like being eighteen again, I always think,' he said.

'That was just what I was thinking!' Caitlin replied.

He put a hand beneath her chin and kissed her lips authoritatively. Taken aback, she pulled quickly away, but Angus seemed unruffled.

'That's to tell you I'm glad we left it until now to meet each other.'

Worries about the ward were instantly replaced by worries about Angus. Caitlin didn't know how she felt about him, she found. Now, sitting in the warm darkness waiting for the main feature film to begin, she felt safe and sure with him. He seemed so often to be in tune with her own thoughts and moods. He had been kind to her while she was so homesick. Maybe Marian was right and he really was serious about her.

But what then? Something inside Caitlin stubbornly refused to yield to him; even to respond to his kisses. He was nice, but that was all that she could feel. She took his compliments, his kindness and his generosity with gratitude, but she could not return his feelings.

Much later, submitting to his embrace, she halfwished she wanted it. He held her quite gently, but there was a tension in him, a latent passion in his kiss that made her push him away.

'Can't I stay? Please, Caitlin?'

He looked so pathetically hopeful. He was always so careful not to hurt her feelings or to offend her. She searched for the right words to reject him without causing him pain, but she could not find them.

'No, Angus,' she said, smoothing her hair, 'please don't ask me that.'

'But why, Caitlin, why?' His voice was pleading, boyish.

'Because I don't want it, that's all, Angus.'

At the door she stared silently at him and he shrugged angrily. She hated sending him off like this, but there was simply no alternative for her.

After he'd gone, she began slowly to undress. Tears filled her eyes, then fell on to the floor. Was it always going to be like this for her? she wondered. She knew she could not bear the thought that she would live alone for ever.

CHAPTER SEVEN

SISTER Fairfield had decided to wait until midday on Monday before notifying the police of Robbie Rae's failure to return to the Unit. All morning she had waited for a telephone call or for the boy to turn up back from his weekend at home. Neither had come.

Staff Nurse O'Connell had failed four times to get a reply when she had telephoned Miss Farrell's holiday home on four occasions, and Jonathan English was like a bear with a sore head.

'I tell you there's no point in waiting any longer,' he growled now for the third time in the hour. 'By the time they find him . . . anything could have happened. What the hell's the matter with you, Ginny?'

'There's nothing the matter with *me*, Dr English,' Sister said coldly. The man was going from bad to worse! 'It's now just before twelve o'clock, and I thought it advisable to give Miss Farrell a reasonable chance of interpreting "morning" liberally.'

'Reasonable!' exploded the physician. 'There's nothing reasonable about that woman!'

'That's as may be, Dr English,' Sister Fairfield stated tartly, 'But *I* am concerned with my patient, and not with his mother!'

It had not been lost on Sister how Dr English and Miss Farrell affected one another, and she had not found the sight an edifying one. She had tolerated their simmering looks and impassioned exchanges only with difficulty. It pained her to see how love ill suited Jonathan English, but at least it had cured her of any

silly notions she might have entertained about the
man.

He gave her a withering look.

'When *are* you going to telephone the police?' he
asked again.

'Right now, Dr English,' Sister replied, 'if you'll
excuse me.'

Caitlin, checking Dangerous Drugs Act listed
preparations at the medicine cupboard, watched Sister
disappear into her room and Dr English into his. She
was pretty certain that they'd been fighting. Everybody seemed to be fighting, she reflected unhappily:
she and Angus, she and Nurse Adrian, Sister and Dr
English, she and Dr English. And it was she who was
the common factor. Ever since she and Robbie
appeared on the Unit . . .

Robbie! He would be all right; he *had* to be all
right. Caitlin glanced up for the hundredth time at the
clock above the nurses' station. It said exactly midday.
Sister had said she would notify the police if he still
wasn't back by midday.

'Staff O'Connell, there's a diabetic diet come up
from the Diet Kitchen extra,' Sister Fairfield's voice
carried an unusually urgent ring. 'I want you to have
it. You can take it in my room. I'll finish here.' She
busied herself immediately with the book which Caitlin
had been using to check the contents of the scheduled
drug cupboard. 'An ambulance crew is getting ready
to go with a police escort in search of Robbie Rae.
I'd like you to accompany them.'

Caitlin ate her lunch in Sister's room, trying to
remain calm. She finished, took her tray back to the
ward kitchen and grabbed her gaberdine from the
cloakroom. It crossed her mind that she might just
have eaten Robbie's lunch. Five minutes later she was
out on the ambulance forecourt outside A & E.

'Staff Nurse UYCS?'

'Yes.'

'This one,'

Caitlin followed the ambulanceman, who seemed to have been awaiting her arrival. He opened the back doors of an ambulance, and she saw that Jonathan was already inside. She took her seat quickly on the opposite side of the vehicle.

She had no sooner done so than the ambulance swung out into the main street. Two police motorcycle outriders joined them and they jumped three sets of traffic lights in succession to bring them out on to the Lothian Road. She watched the unfamiliar shopping parades of Bruntsfield and Morningside flash past from the dark interior of the ambulance. The journey was smoother than any she had ever experienced. It was the first time she had travelled like this, and she could not decide whether the experience was a pleasant or an extremely unpleasant one.

She avoided meeting Jonathan English's eyes. She was not unduly surprised to find herself sharing this mission with him, but it was not easy to sit in the confined, dusky space of the ambulance with him.

Gradually, coherent thoughts began to surface above her anxiety over Robbie. She remembered the scene on Friday afternoon and the speculation she had struggled with all through the weekend. So Jonathan had not spent his days off with Penelope Farrell. Or not all of them, anyway.

If he had been there, this would not have happened; of that much she felt sure. She looked for the first time full at the man opposite her, and found his eyes on her face.

'What are you thinking about?' he demanded brusquely.

Caitlin was glad of the cover the darkened interior of the ambulance offered. She said nothing.

'Your love-life?' he sneered.

She stared bitterly across at the physician and hoped he could see the contempt that glittered in her eyes. Perhaps he did, because he seemed to recoil from what he had just said.

'I saw you at the cinema,' he explained, trying to normalise his voice.

Caitlin smiled a painful half-smile. So that was it!

'Did you indeed?' she asked with dignity.

The ambulance chose that moment to bump to a halt, and they got out into the damp grey mist that rolled down the brownish hillsides into the valley. There was not a soul nor a building in sight, but a rough lane disappeared into the mist from the corner of the layby where they had stopped.

Caitlin started up the hill behind Jonathan and the ambulance crew, while the motorcycle outriders strode on ahead. Jonathan seemed to know the way. Caitlin reminded herself of Friday. He'd probably accompanied Miss Farrell and Robbie all the way to the cottage, even if it wasn't drivable, she reflected, then gone to the cinema. Well, she had nothing to be ashamed of. What business of his was it that she went to see a film with Angus Dougan?

She pictured Jonathan walking up here with Robbie, reassuring him, telling him to have a nice time. He would talk to him like that, she knew. As a doctor and as a man he was both thorough and kind. Thorough and kind and . . . loving. She stopped her train of thought. One minute she was safely thinking about her right to go out with whom she pleased, and the next she was dreaming. She chided herself into a miserable mental silence and tightened the belt of her gaberdine raincoat against the cold—or against a strange hunger she could not name.

Suddenly she had to restrain herself from running up behind Jonathan and catching his arm. Here they both were in search of their lost patient. But what about their lost past? What, she suddenly longed to ask, about their lost future?

She had fallen far behind and, as if aware of her missing behind him, the physician stopped and waited for her to catch up with him. She was almost calm by the time she did so and her wild emotions were under control once more.

'That's better,' he murmured, as she took her place by him.

The cottage appeared out of the mist a few seconds later—a low stone building in a copse of fir trees. It seemed deserted and ghostly in the misty darkness of the wood. A barbed wire fence had been stretched across the path ahead of them to put off intruders, and Jonathan held it up for Caitlin to crawl underneath.

Standing up again next to him, she noticed how pale he was. She felt a sudden stab of pity for him, she did not know why. It was Robbie who deserved and needed all her pity now, wherever he was. If he was up here, he would be greatly in need of care when he was found. If he was found.

She stumbled across the uneven turf towards the little house, while her medical colleague ran round to the back of it. Caitlin was not surprised when the front door was found to be locked. She cupped her hands and tried to look in through the grimy window-panes of the downstairs rooms, but lace curtaining obscured her view.

One of the policemen rang twice at the front door, trying to force the lock with no effect. And then he unceremoniously kicked it in with two blows of his booted foot.

'Two upstairs, two down,' he instructed.

One of the ambulancemen and a policeman mounted the picturesque spiral staircase while Caitlin stayed on the ground floor with the other two, uncertain of her own rôle. She had time to look about her.

Everything was totally still. The cottage felt cold
and unlived-in. It was almost exactly as Caitlin had
imagined. Once, the humble little house must have
cosily contained a shepherd and his family. Now, in
spite of all the money that had been spent on it, it felt
unloved and bleak.

It had been turned into a luxurious retreat for the
rich, but it felt as though it would rather have been
left as it was, however dilapidated. The expensive
rustic furniture was mildewed, the carpet stained with
damp.

Above Caitlin's head, the heavy tread of the
searching men stopped, having a similar effect on her
heart. Jonathan appeared too, his suit mud-bespat-
tered and his shirt out at the back. His face, though,
conveyed total control.

'There's no sign of him out there,' he said, 'nor in
the wood. But there's one possibility.'

He hurtled past her and up the spiral staircase two
steps at a time. She followed him, slightly more
demurely but scarcely more quiet inside.

'This way.'

He led her right along the upstairs corridor, which
ran the width of the house. At the far end of it, the
other searchers were reviewing the possibilities of
widening the search to the surrounding woods and
countryside. Jonathan pushed past them, opening a
door into a tiny end bedroom.

'There's an attic,' he said.

The attic trapdoor would never have been found by
anyone who did not know the house well, Caitlin
reflected. It was above a wardrobe, hidden completely
from casual view and obviously out of use for many
years.

Jonathan pushed the wardrobe out of the way and
pulled an old oak dresser over until he could stand on

it below the attic door. He got up, pushed aside the trapdoor with difficulty, and heaved himself up into the darkness.

Caitlin was left waiting with the others, but to her the time seemed infinite.

'Are you all right up there, Dr English, sir?' One of the ambulance crew asked the question that was in her mind. The other one glanced at his wrist watch and muttered 'twelve forty-five' under his breath.

Twelve forty-five: three-quarters of an hour since Robbie's lunchtime—and how many meals had he missed by now? If his body was still quietly producing insulin he might be all right. If his 'honeymoon period' was holding fast, he would be fine. But if not . . . Caitlin confined herself to praying that the boy was okay.

There was the sound of something being dragged, perhaps on a blanket, above them, then some plaster fell in a dusty shower into the room in which they stood. For a second, she thought the whole ceiling was going to fall in on them all.

Then the strained features of Jonathan English appeared in the hatch above them.

'We'll need the stretcher,' he said. 'If one of you can stand directly below, I'll try to lower him gently down. It's the only way to get him out.'

The two policemen left the room while the ambulance crew helped the doctor. Robbie was lowered carefully through the trapdoor and down into the ambulancemen's arms. One of them carried the unconscious boy swiftly along and down the spiral staircase with a fireman's lift, as the stairs were too steep to negotiate with a stretcher. At the bottom, Robbie was transferred to a portable canvas stretcher and the journey back down the hill began.

Caitlin was not sorry to hear the cottage door being boarded up behind them by the police. Sleet began to

slant down on the procession which wound its way
down the lane, and Caitlin pulled the blanket up over
Robbie until only his eyes were visible beneath the
tangled halo of his golden hair at the top of the
stretcher.

Once inside the ambulance, she uncovered him and
at last allowed herself a sigh of relief as Jonathan
examined him. Robbie was flushed and Caitlin could
smell acetone on his breath once more, but he was
not so deeply unconscious as he had been on his first
admission to the RCH.

It was hard to tell how long he had lain without
food or drink, but his 'honeymoon' was clearly over
now. That had been short and far from sweet, Caitlin
reflected grimly, but surely now he would be free to
stabilise without further incident.

'No bones broken,' said Jonathan, 'miraculously.'

He quickly and faultlessly found a vein, took blood
for analysis as soon as they reached the RCH, and
put up a drip with Ringer's solution.

'The rafters are rotten up there. He could have
fallen much more badly, through the plaster into the
downstairs room,' the physician said, almost as if
talking to himself. 'He must have got in through the
skylight from the roof—it's always open. A barn owl
has been nesting up there. They always come back to
the same place each year. Robbie must have been told
and gone up looking for her.'

Caitlin listened dully to his words, resisting what
they implied. She took Robbie's pulse and respirations, then tested his pupils, which reacted quite briskly
to her torchlight. She tried to concentrate on him to
the exclusion of the consultant.

As the ambulance swung back into the compound
in front of A & E, Robbie became restless, plucking
at the wrist Jonathan had used for the drip and
mumbling inarticulate words. Caitlin spoke to the boy

quietly, urgently, trying to orientate him and bring him up. All the way through the casualty department and up to UYCS she saw and heard nothing but the changes in Robbie's level of consciousness.

She cleared the locker top of the pop magazines and tapes which had littered it and replaced them with a covered tray of resuscitation equipment. Then began half-hourly recordings and a new fluid balance sheet. All the time she kept an eye on Robbie, watching and alert for the smallest improvement in his condition.

He seemed unable to rouse himself, though for nearly an hour, ever since he had been brought down from the attic, he had been on the brink of consciousness.

Sister Fairfield looked in and Caitlin gave her a full report. This served only to supplement the full picture of the situation provided her by Dr English, and the assessment she made herself now. She knew the boy was in the best possible hands and that the nursing care he was receiving was the best she could provide. Sister did not exclude herself from this observation; there was no overestimating her new staff nurse.

'And no sign of Mum?' she asked.

Caitlin shook her head. She and Sister exchanged looks which conveyed more than any words could.

'What is the world coming to?' the older nurse asked the boy who lay between them. 'Staff, stay with him until you go off. I'll look again soon. If you need me I'll be in a doctors' meeting until two, then around and about.'

And so the long uphill fight began again. It was like a dream which repeats itself, perfect in every detail, on a second occasion. But this time Caitlin knew her patient. She knew his whims, his way, his bodily response to glucose and insulin. And although no two roads to recovery ever followed exactly the same path, she found it much easier, having come the way before with him, to help him through.

She hardly noticed Jonathan come in, shutting the door softly behind him. She was so absorbed in her work that she soon forgot him again, standing motionless and silent beside the window from where he watched her.

Once he said he was waiting for blood results.

'We'll give him some more glucose when I've seen them,' he added.

When the haematology results came he drew up the glucose himself and added it to the Ringer's solution on the drip stand.

'Thank you,' said Caitlin, noting the addition and the time on the label of the bottle.

Once he coughed while she was counting a pulse and made her jump, so that she had to start all over again.

All afternoon she moved through her ritual recordings and care, always encouraging Robbie with words and touch. And all afternoon the consultant monitored her every move while Robbie struggled to the surface.

Just before she was due to go off duty at four, he opened his eyes. She pushed his hair back from his brow and stroked him softly.

'About time too,' she whispered. 'Jamie's been asking for you, young Robbie Rae. You're back on the Unit safe and sound, and everything's going to be okay.'

She picked up one of the charts on his bedtable to note his return to consciousness and the time. When she looked up, she saw that Jonathan was smiling for the first time in, it seemed, years.

'I'm off now, Dr English,' she said more matter-of-factly than she felt. 'So I hope you'll excuse me. Someone will be in any moment to take my place.'

'That won't be possible,' he murmured almost

inaudibly, 'but . . .'

Staff Nurse Harrison arrived at the second to relieve Caitlin.

' . . . thank you.'

It was a cold clear afternoon. All trace of sleet and snow had vanished, banished by a colder wind, but Caitlin was warmed by two tiny words which radiated heat inside her.

She tripped along the pavement amongst the duffle-coated students, hardly feeling her feet touch the ground. He had thanked her, and his thanks meant more to her than all the compliments ever paid her by Angus Dougan. He had thanked her, and she felt as though they were the only thanks she could ever need again, for anything.

It was a ridiculous feeling, but it was true. She patted the little stone dog on his pedestal outside the pub which bore his name: Greyfriars Bobby. Bobby had lain on his dead master's grave, refusing to budge, and had been commemorated for his loyalty and love.

She told the story over to herself as she walked down towards the Royal Mile, spring in her step. She turned down towards Holyrood Park, determined to climb Arthur's Seat and see the view from the top of the hill. It was a little outing she had promised herself before now, and today was so clear that the view would be perfect.

She took a path through the park which crossed a burn via a little wooden bridge. Some sheep scuttled out of her way and stood looking bemused, watching her climb up the eight hundred feet towards the summit of the hill.

The view was all that she had hoped for. She thought of Robbie, looking out over the Firth of Forth, the small fishing villages and harbours all clearly visible from here. Robbie was safe, and the world looked wonderful. The two seemed to go hand in hand.

She looked down on the palace of Holyrood House nestling amongst its trees and felt herself as much mistress of all that she surveyed as the Queen. She might not own a palace or a park, but Robbie was safe and she had had a hand in his recovery.

For the first time that day, Caitlin thought about how Jonathan English had been involved all the way through, just as she had been. For the first time it seemed odd to her how he had waited in his room all afternoon, as if he had nothing else to do. But what more could he do?

That was the limitation of medicine. Just when the patient most needed you, you were gone; your rôle was fulfilled. After the diagnosis and the prescription the doctor's work was done—while hers was just beginning.

Insulin and glucose therapy had played their part in Robbie's care and in his recovery, but it was good nursing which had pulled him through. She did not feel proud or conceited. She just knew it, and, more significantly, she knew that Jonathan had known it too. That was what she celebrated, looking out over her new domain.

At long last, something was settled between her and Jonathan. At long last she was his equal. She was no longer an ex-patient, a junior nurse, a mere nobody. She had shown him who she was, and they were quits.

She pulled her collar up and waited until a ship had made the safety of the far harbour. Her superstitious mind again! Then she ran down the hill, arriving breathless and lighthearted as a child among the startled sheep.

'Surprise!'

The more sedate walk back to Cathcart Street had sobered but not subdued her, so she was quite pleased to find Angus waiting for her at the front door. It was the first time she had seen him since the post-cinema scene—off duty anyway—and she was even more glad to have that behind them.

'What do you want?' she asked mischievously. 'Not a bed for the night, I hope?'

'Hmm!' returned Angus thoughtfully. 'I'll let that pass, I think. How about a meal?'

Caitlin agreed. They jumped into his old car and made off. She noted with mild interest that they were taking precisely the same route taken earlier by the ambulance. But that journey seemed now to belong to another world, another lifetime.

'Big drama today, I hear,' remarked Angus. 'And you're the heroine, it seems.'

'Oh, no!' She was genuinely upset at the suggestion. 'Not at all. Robbie's the hero. Or Dr English. He was quite brave, getting him out.'

Angus gave her an old-fashioned look.

'Well,' he said, 'it depends on who's telling this story, it seems.'

Caitlin wasn't sure she understood that remark, so she let it lie.

It was nearly six by the time they pulled up outside a country inn. The road sign nearby, which she could just make out in the darkness, said 'Easter Howgate'—a funny name, she thought. She had no idea where they were, but the hills around them were dark and desolate and she was glad to get inside the pub.

The bar was beautifully kept, with glowing brass beer taps, sparkling glasses and a roaring log fire. Caitlin sat and thought about doctors while Angus got them a drink. She watched the flames reflected in a big copper preserving pan which hung in the ingle-nook.

She was glad she had become a nurse. There was a perfect balance between a nurse and a doctor, she thought. One cured and one cared, and occasionally the two got miraculously combined. She could not help her mind straying to the particular. Jonathan, she knew, combined his gifts in medicine. He too knew how to care, as she had once found out, never to forget.

The euphoria of the afternoon faded. Why had he not been able to either help or go away this afternoon? Was it simply his seniority now that stopped him from caring as he had once cared for her? Yes, that must be it. Even Angus was closer to the patient now than he would be when he reached consultancy. And yet something did not ring true. Dr Sass was adored by all his patients. He had not allowed seniority to come between him and them.

There must be something else. He had been in charge of the rescue today. If he had not been there, would they have found Robbie? Caitlin doubted it. It did not bear thinking about. His first aid and instant insulin injection had begun Robbie on the road to recovery. She knew that . . .

'I don't think we'll have the trouble here we had at the Italian place,' Angus thrust a menu into her hand and put her drink down in front of her.

Sipping her special diabetic drink, she recalled the trouble she had had finding something on the menu there which she could eat. Scanning this menu, she saw that it couldn't have been more different.

The entire menu was made up of a list of varied smörrebröd, Danish delicacies laid on pieces of thinly buttered breads. There was everything from caviar to prawns, from egg to cheese and rare roast beef. They took their time to choose, and Caitlin selected four different things which together made up her allowance of exchanges for this time of day.

'A bit unusual for a pub in the Pentland Hills, isn't it?' asked Angus. He paused, mid-bite of smoked salmon.

Caitlin nodded appreciatively. She was surprised to find they were in the Pentlands for the second time that day.

'It's very well known. You can't get in here for love nor money at the weekends. Many a time I've brought someone down to impress them and got turned out on my ear!'

She smiled.

'So it's just as well as we got in this evening,' he went on, 'as there's nobody I'd rather impress—at the moment anyway.'

She nodded again, this time with comprehension.

'I see,' she said. 'How kind!'

They ate in companionable silence for a time. A local old man came in and heaved himself up on to a bar stool, then balanced his sheep's-head crook beside him against the bar. The landlord welcomed him. It must be nice for the locals when their pub wasn't full of strangers from the city, Caitlin thought, and they could enjoy a pint in peace.

'Usual, Lachlan?'

'Aye, that'll do.'

A pint of thick black beer was placed before him, and he supped in silence for a minute or two.

'A fine carry-on today, was it no'?' He put his empty pint back down on the bar carefully. 'Up at the auld bothy?'

The landlord leaned confidentially over the bar on one elbow.

'Aye,' he agreed, 'that it was. Another?'

'Ha' ain yoursel',' said the old man.

The two resettled themselves in front of their drinks.

'She'll come to no guid, that lassie, mind.'

'That's what you always said, Lachlan.'

'They say she left the laddie alane up there while she went off wi' one of her men.'

'Is that right?' the landlord said soberly.

Caitlin's ears pricked. They had to be talking about Robbie.

'That's a bad un, that one. I mind when she was just a wee bairn, and she was a rum one them. Always got her ain way, that was the bother. They were a right odd lot, they Farrells. I always said so, right when we sold them the bothy, wi' a' their airs and graces an' a'. But the lassie, she was the worst.'

'She's in here a lot, you know,' confided the landlord. 'She was in the other week wi' a fellow. A good-looking young fellow, he was too, wi' a right posh accent, I mind. An Englishman, I'd say.'

'Weel,' the old local rejoined without respect, 'they Sassenachs deserve a' they get. An' he'll get plenty frae her!'

Caitlin did not feel hungry any more. She ate the last of her smörrebröd without relish and sat allowing the conversation she had overheard to sink in. It served her right for listening in, she thought. She well deserved all the misery it brought her.

It brought her plenty. She was plunged into morbid contemplation of Penelope Farrell and Jonathan English enjoying a romantic fireside supper here, perhaps in the very two seats she and Angus now occupied. She shifted uncomfortably in her chair.

'Okay? Was that good?' asked Angus, a puzzled frown on his face at her faraway expression.

'Oh yes, super, thanks, Angus. I was just . . . getting a little hot,' she said.

'We could move? There's a nice empty cosy corner over there.

'Oh, no, this is fine, honestly. It's lovely by the fire.'

'We used to have an open fire in Perth in the old days . . .'

Angus's voice droned on while Caitlin tortured herself with her own imagination. And of course, Jonathan had indeed known the cottage. They probably came down here in the evenings, ate and went back up together . . . She could not bear it. She simply could not bear it.

It was so unlike the Jonathan English she had once known: so correct, so aware of his ethical responsibilitlies. How could he let himself get involved with a relative of one of his own patients? It must be an overwhelming affair, she decided miserably, an overwhelming passion . . .

She stopped. It was too much, even for her.

CHAPTER EIGHT

CAITLIN awoke early and caught a bus up to the RCH. She liked to get in early when she was in charge. Things had a knack of storing themselves up for Sister Fairfield's day off, she'd discovered, and she didn't see why today should be any exception.

Angus collared her the minute she set foot on the Unit, and she remembered with irritation his lingering kiss the night before.

'You're holding the fort today?' he asked.

Now what? she thought.

'I am,' she said.

'And what about tonight?'

'What about it?'

He chucked her affectionately beneath the chin.

'Got out of bed the wrong side this morning?' he asked.

Caitlin felt even more irritated.

'Listen, do you know what the date is today? January the twenty-fifth,' Angus informed her pleasantly, 'the birthday of our great and celebrated bard. Robert Burns—for the benefit of you—er—other Celts.'

Caitlin allowed herself to be softened a little by his obviously happy mood.

'Oh, yes?' she said. 'Robert Burns what?'

'I'll let that pass too. I'm planning a surprise party, a Burns Night supper, at Marian's. That's the surprise —she doesn't know yet! More fun than the normal residency do. Just a few close friends. What do you think?'

Caitlin wasn't quite sure what a Burns Night Supper might entail, and she was still wondering about it when Angus changed the subject completely, saying that he'd just come off the phone to Penelope Farrell.

'She just called to make sure the laddie was back "safe and sound",' Angus imitated a cultured English accent rather rudely.

Caitlin's surprise must have shown in her face.

'Is that all she said?' she managed at last. 'No explanations? Nothing?'

'Oh, she'd plenty explanations by the time I'd finished with her,' Angus assured her. 'An' I expect she'll have cooked up a few more by the time Sass speaks to her this afternoon.'

Yes, Caitlin thought bitterly, I bet she will, too.

'She will be up here "by the first available flight",' Angus minced again.

'Flight? Where on earth is she?' asked Caitlin.

'Why, in her London apartment, of course, where she arrived on Sunday night late, in preparation for an audition on Monday morning early.'

She stared at him in disbelief.

'You mean she left Robbie on his own . . .' she began slowly and carefully.

Nurse Adrian appeared in the Unit doorway, her beret askew and her hair escaping from beneath it. Glancing covertly at the staff nurse and SHO, the student disappeared into the cloakroom as if she had just been caught stealing the Crown Jewels. Caitlin drew Angus into Sister's room where they could not be overheard.

'She left him in the cottage alone?' she reiterated.

'That's right. Well, he'd been well enough all weekend and she'd no reason to believe he couldn't cope for a few hours on his own. She couldn't cancel her audition, not at such short notice, and besides, it was a big part. She'd given the boy his taxi fare back to the hospital for Monday morning. What more could she do?'

Caitlin was speechless.

Angus shrugged. 'Well,' he said at last, 'I suppose there's mothers and mothers.'

'Anyway,' he added, 'I'm off to take bloods. And Caitlin—I'm letting Davy Selkirk home today. His family want him there, and it's as good as anywhere for him now . . .'

Caitlin nodded mutely. The meaning of that was plain enough, anyway. It meant there was nothing more that the Unit could do for him.

'I'll make sure he's ready,' she said softly. 'What time are they coming for him?'

'Around two,' Angus replied. He gave her a long look. 'Chin up, lassie!' he said.

Nurse Adrian looked exhausted. It was only two weeks until she sat State and tomorrow she would be moving to the Renal Unit. She looked as if she hadn't slept properly in weeks, and Caitlin's heart went out to her.

'Have you been studying hard?' she asked the student when they'd finished giving out the breakfasts. 'You look awfully tired.'

'I'm okay,' the girl replied sullenly.

'Well, we're not too busy this morning. I'll take the Professor's ward round if you look after his three patients. You can take the first-year with you and I'll keep the second-year with me.' Caitlin had sent the two younger nurse learners to bath one of the iller patients.

She felt at a loss how to cope with Nurse Adrian's continuing hostility and had decided simply to stick it out as best she could until the girl left the Unit. In fact, as time went by, she found her patience increased rather than the other way around.

She remembered only too well how it felt to be on top of State Registration examinations. One's whole future was in the balance, and it seemed impossible to revise all that once had been so fresh in one's mind. All the lectures, all the clinical instruction—all had to be gone over and remembered.

Caitlin had been reduced to tears of hopeless conviction that nothing she had revised would come up in the exams. And then when she had been faced with the paper and discovered she could answer all the questions—what sweet relief! Yes, she sympathised with Nurse Adrian.

Nevertheless, it would be better when she had left the Unit. It was not much fun to be constantly snubbed and to anticipate her sulky response to every request made of her. Caitlin sat down at her paperwork with resignation. It was important to have a good staffing post to go to. That was what had carried her through in the end: the fact that she knew she had a job here waiting for her when she passed. It was all the incentive she'd required.

She wondered for a moment, closing the Kardex, where she would go from here. She didn't really want to go into nursing administration, although that was where the money was and where her logical mind could easily carry her. Suddenly, the clinical nursing specialist on the Renal Unit flashed into her head. That was the sort of post she'd love. She must remember to ask Sister about the possibility for that diabetic support job she'd mentioned . . .

Caitlin was interrupted by the appearance of Professor Carstairs. Or rather, she was interrupted by the reverent hush which seemed always to herald his appearance on the Unit. She glanced round and there, sure enough, he stood, surrounded by his white-coated flock. He frowned and waited for her to respond to his presence.

This she did. The entourage was large this morning and the Professor was in his element, living up to his image as diligent doctor-in-chief. It occurred to Caitlin that he was one of a dying breed. The younger men did not carry their responsibilities with such gravity. They were more approachable, more like Dr English . . .

'When you're ready, Staff Nurse O'Connell.'

'I'll be with you now, Professor Carstairs.'

She fetched the trolley full of medical notes and followed the entourage to the first bed. Nurse Adrian was making it around the patient and she showed no sign of stopping for the round.

It was annoying to have to tell her publicly to do what she already knew. But Caitlin had to do it, and she was rewarded with an insolent shrug and a shy, quick, nervous smile from the first-year.

She silently screened the patient.

The Professor was in loquacious mood. Angus glanced several times at Caitlin, trying to catch her eye, especially on the once or twice that familiar anecdotes cropped up in the Professor's speech. But she kept her eyes averted and her mind on the job. If Angus felt the Professor had nothing more to teach him, she did not share his feeling.

Still, it was galling to spend quite such an age on so few patients, especially when it was not the patients who were benefiting—directly anyway—from the lengthy conversations round their beds.

It was amazing what patients suffered in the cause of medical science—and nursing science, if it came to that. Caitlin tried to recall all the smiling faces who had agreed to be 'case studies', who had accompanied her to case conferences and who had obediently taken off their pyjama jacket for the umpteenth time that

day while yet another young doctor or nurse examined
them.

She manipulated her trolley around the door of
Robbie's side room and was beside his bed before she
wondered what on earth they were all doing there.
Surely he still wasn't being seen by both medical
chiefs?

The Professor's manner changed. He obviously had
a soft spot for 'the Rae boy'. Caitlin looked to Angus
for explanation, but for once the SHO seemed quite
unwilling to meet her eye.

'And how are we today?' the Professor asked pleasantly.

'No' too bad,' Robbie replied economically.

Caitlin felt he could be more polite to the great
man, but once more she sensed her young patient
bristling with rebellion. It did not take long for Robbie
Rae to be back in fighting form, she thought wryly.

'I hear our little experiment went somewhat awry,'
encouraged the Professor. When he still got no
response he turned unperturbed to his entourage and
explained at length about Robbie's 'honeymoon period'
and its aftermath. 'In short,' he concluded, 'it was a
very brief remission and young Rae here has been
more than happy to accept his insulin from us again,
haven't you, Robbie?'

'I suppose so.' Robbie spoke into his lap.

'Are there any questions?'

Professor Carstairs patted the boy paternally on the
head and gazed over his glasses at the rapt faces of
his students.

'Why isn't Dr Sassenach coming to see me any
more?'

There was a silence during which everybody focused
their attention on Robbie. He stared resolutely at the
Professor, awaiting his reply.

'Well now, young fellow,' the Professor said, flushing

slightly, his reply.

Caitlin held her breath. There was no doubt that the Professor was annoyed. And what was Robbie talking about? True, she had not seen Jonathan near his room in the last few hours—in fact, she hadn't seen him at all this morning. But there was nothing too unusual in that. He often spent the morning on the Renal Unit, his other area of medical responsibility. Or at a meeting, or something.

Still the boy and the Professor faced one another and Robbie did not flinch.

'I expect there's some very good reason for that, now don't you? I expect there's some good reason for my seeing you instead.' The Professor was definitely very put out.

'I dunno,' pouted Robbie. 'I like Dr Sassenach.'

An uncomfortable, embarrassed ripple of amusement ran through the assembled doctors on the round, and Caitlin found herself willing her young patient to be quiet. This was turning into a decidedly unpleasant scene.

'Yes, well, I'm sure you do, young man. We all have our preferences, don't we?'

He swept out of the room, leaving Robbie without a backward glance. The entourage followed and Caitlin came out last to receive her ritual thanks for the ward round. The minute she had done so, she ran back into Robbie's room, where she found him in tears.

'What on earth came over you, Robbie?' she asked, putting her arm around him.

He sobbed loudly and then wiped his nose on the tissue she handed him.

'I like Dr Sassenach,' he repeated pathetically.

'Yes, I know,' comforted Caitlin. It was awful to see him so upset.

'Well, why has he given up coming to see me? Is he annoyed with me?'

'No, of course not, Robbie,' she whispered, holding him close.

He submitted for a second, then struggled free of her arms, his anger surfacing through his tears.

'Jamie says he'll no' see me any more because I got sick over the weekend,' he muttered.

Caitlin was surprised and shocked.

'That's not true, Robbie! Listen, if you sit quietly, then eat your lunch, I'll find out what's happened and come back and tell you as soon as I can. How would that be?'

He nodded dumbly. Caitlain let herself out of the room straight into an eavesdropper.

'Jamie! What are you doing? I want a word with you!'

Jamie looked most uncomfortable. She took him firmly by the arm and led him into Sister's room, where she closed the door behind them.

'Now, Jamie, what's all this you've been telling Robbie?'

'It's true,' Jamie said quickly, hardly daring to meet her eyes.

'What's true?' she demanded quietly.

'Dr Sass is no' Robbie's doctor ony mair.'

'And what makes you so sure of that?'

He stared at the floor without answering.

'Did you hear me, Jamie? I want to know.'

'From the notes.'

The reading of case notes were one of Jamie's better-rehearsed pranks, and all the nursing staff had been warned about it. It was strictly forbidden and gave him a position of power over other patients, both of which he thrived on.

'So you've been reading the case notes again, have you, Jamie?'

'Aye.'

She waited patiently for an apology for him. She

hadn't noticed anything in the notes which could have given the boy such an idea, but she had hardly had time to glance at them, what with the scene during the recent Professorial ward round.

As if he read her thoughts, Jamie looked up.

'There's a letter,' he said, 'at the back.'

'You're really very naughty, Jamie. You made Robbie really miserable. Do you know that?'

Jamie looked very unhappy himself at this.

'I'm sorry—honest.'

'Okay, Jamie, you can go and have your lunch now. And no more reading notes. Okay?'

'Okay,' he muttered.

Caitlin checked the diabetic diets that had come up from the Diet Kitchen. She took a tempting pudding off Robbie's tray and replaced it with fruit. They were very clever at producing sweets without sugar in them, but it was really much kinder to let Robbie get used to simpler fare to begin with. Also, Mrs Rae would be limited in what she could produce for him until she got used to cooking slightly differently for him.

Poor Robbie! She would have to find out what was happening to his medical care and tell him the truth. Nothing ever went smoothly for him for long, it seemed. It was ridiculous that he should feel that Jonathan was angry with him. She would have to sort it all out.

She said goodbye to Davy Selkirk at the Unit doors a short time later. The cheery porter who had come up with a wheelchair to help Mrs Selkirk collect her husband was full of good advice.

'Don't you miss him, nurse,' he told Caitlin, 'he's away to a party tonight. Isn't that right, Mr Selkirk?'

Davy Selkirk held his wife's hand and grinned up at Caitlin.

'That's right. We're having a wee party to oursel's tonight, aren't we, Jeannie?'

His wife returned his smile.

'It's Burns Night, the night, nurse. That's what he means.'

'Well, I hope you have a lovely evening,' Caitlin told them both. 'And all our best wishes go with you, Mr Selkirk.'

It was hard to say goodbye to him, and Caitlin was glad to feel the familiar stocky presence of Angus suddenly at her side.

'Good luck, Mr Selkirk,' he said, shaking his patient firmly by the hand and smiling at Mrs Selkirk too. 'Good luck to both of you,' he added gently.

They left, and, turning back into the Unit, Caitlin struggled to refocus her mind.

'Oh, Angus, there's something I must speak to you about.'

She followed him into the doctors' room and he waited for her to speak, gazing wearily out of the window as if temporarily defeated. Perhaps, she thought, Mr Selkirk in her mind, that's exactly how he's feeling. She found it difficult to break the silence, but at last she found her tongue.

'It's about Robbie Rae,' she said. 'He's got some crazy notion in his head that Dr English isn't coming up to see him any more. It seems ridiculous, but . . .'

'It isn't ridiculous,' said Angus tiredly. 'Dr English won't be seeing him any more. Professor Carstairs will be seeing him from now on.'

'But . . .' Caitlin intervened, astonished, 'he's . . . I mean, Dr English . . .'

'He's been taken off the case,' he told her curtly.

'Taken off the case?' she repeated with dull shock.

'That's what I said,' replied Angus, irritated. 'Dr English has been taken off that particular case and is no longer responsible for his medical care.'

He shuffled some papers on his desk, evidently annoyed by her continued presence in the room.

'Would you mind, Caitlin?' he said eventually. 'I'm
very busy right now. I'll see you this evening. Okay?'

Caitlin's first concern was how to tell Robbie Rae. It
was all very well these decisions being made by the
medical powers that be, but what about the patient?
It was hard to guess how this might affect Robbie.

He adored 'Dr Sassenach'. It was a blatant understatement when the child said that he 'liked' the
doctor. He was as much of a hero-worshipper of the
consultant as any of the other young patients. Jamie
and Robbie both quoted the physician as an overall
authority on all matters from medical to social
—Caitlin had heard them. She dreaded to think how
Robbie would react to the fact that he was no longer
under the care of the Englishman.

She paused outside Robbie's room, then went in.
They boy was lying on his bed staring at the ceiling,
his lunch still unfinished on the tray beside him.

'Robbie,' she began softly. 'you must eat your fruit.
You haven't had enough to eat yet for lunch. Would
you prefer biscuits and cheese?'

'No.'

'Well, eat up your banana, then. Please. I want to
tell you something.'

Robbie sulkily began to peel his fruit and slowly
bite pieces off it.

'I've spoken to Dr Dougan, Robbie, and it seems
that you'll be seen by the Professor from now on. He's
a very important man, Robbie, and he cares about
you very much.'

Robbie finished his banana in total silence.

'Professor Carstairs is very nice, Robbie. He only
pretends to be strict sometimes, just for people's own
good.'

Caitlin did not sound as if she believed in her own

reasoning. Of course, it was true that the Professor was a dear and that he would care for the boy with undoubted skill and excellence—but that was not the point.

Robbie looked at her as if he read her thoughts. If was as if he was waiting for her to come up with better reasons than that. And she couldn't.

'I liked Dr Sassenach,' he said at last.

Her heart contracted. The past tense was so sad, and there was nothing more that she could say.

'Why don't you go down to the day-room, Robbie? It's nice and sunny and warm down there, and I think Jamie was in there last time I looked. You could listen to some music, or watch the TV.'

Robbie got up heavily, slid off the bed and made for the door. He didn't speak to her again all afternoon.

Ironically, Caitlin's next task was to telephone Margot Rae to give her one of her routine bulletins on Robbie's progress. Mrs Rae had been kept up to date with the dramatic happenings of the weekend and had taken it all with her usual placid good sense.

Caitlin decided it was not up to her to convey the news of the change of medical supervision of Robbie's case to her. She did not have the information to do it; it was up to the doctors. So she made her phone call, passed on the news of Robbie's improved physical condition and left the rest.

After the call, she treated herself to a cup of tea in Sister's room. Today had been just about as hectic as it could have been. And why had Angus been so close? That was typical of the medical profession, Caitlin thought with rancour. They could be as pleasant and open as they liked as long as everything was going smoothly, but the minute anything untoward happened they closed ranks like books on a library shelf and you couldn't get between them for anything.

She sat and counted the minutes until she should get back on to the Unit, wishing she could just walk off duty now. She was tired and depressed by the news Angus had given her and with all that was going on around her, unable to make any sense of it.

Back at the nurses' station, she sent the junior staff to tea and began to tidy up in preparation for going off. There were the nursing notes for Mr Selkirk to complete and file and final notes to be added to the Kardex. She had just begun the latter task when the appearance of Penelope Farrell dispersed what little calm was left in her.

Miss Farrell did not ask to be admitted to the ward, nor had she rung the bell at the outer door, although it was stated on a notice outside that relatives and visitors should please ring before entering. She was dressed in a three-piece tweed suit of masculine design and wore her hair up underneath a matching trilby hat. The effect was quite stunning, and she was dramatically distraught.

'Oh, nurse! Have you seen Professor Carstairs? Where's Robbie? Can I see him now?' She removed her tight leather gloves delicately, then shook her hair free from beneath the hat. 'I've just arrived this minute from Turnhouse airport—I got here the moment I could. Is he all right?'

Caitlin demurred. She was pleased Robbie had acted on her suggestion and was listening to his tape machine in the day-room. The less he heard or saw of his mother in this state of nerves, the better.

'He's fine, Miss Farrell. Would you like a cup of tea? It's just made for the patients and I'm sure I could find you a cup, after your journey?'

'That's sweet of you, nurse, but could I see Professor Carstairs? I *am* so concerned about Robbie . . .'

'I'm sure you are, Miss Farrell,' said Caitlin, ushering her into Sister's room. 'I'll see if I can get hold of the Professor for you, but I know he teaches at another hospital this afternoon.'

She poured Miss Farrell the last cup of tea from the flask in Sister's room, just to distract her for a few more moments. Meanwhile, Miss Farrell wanted to know if she could smoke again. While Caitlin found her an ashtray she had a definite sense of *déjà vu*. But more worrying was the renewed feeling that she was in the presence of a consummate actress who never knew when to come off the stage.

'When you feel ready you can go down and see Robbie,' she told her. 'He's in the day-room, I think. Or shall I ask him to come up back to his room? You'd have more privacy there. Whichever you'd prefer?'

'Oh, I don't mind. I'll go down to the day-room,' Miss Farrell responded vaguely. 'Nurse,' she added suddenly as an apparent afterthought, 'Robbie's fond of you, isn't he?'

Caitlin was taken aback.

'Well, yes, I suppose so. I think he likes several of the nurses,' she said.

'But you're his special favourite?' Miss Farrell persisted.

Caitlin just sat and waited for what was to come next.

'I want you to do something for me, nurse. I know you'll agree—for Robbie's sake. I need to talk to someone about him. Will you meet me somewhere away from here? On neutral territory? Hospital walls have ears. You could come to the British Caledonian Hotel? This evening, at eight? I'm simply frantic to talk to somebody, and you're always so sympathetic, and I know Robbie loves you—he's told me so.'

Penelope Farrell gave Caitlin a look which suggested she was not altogether thrilled with this fact. Then her expression changed to one of imploring.

'Please, nurse! Only you can help me. You must understand!'

'Well, very well, Miss Farrell. If you insist . . .' Caitlin simply did not know what else she could say.

'That's settled, then.' Penelope Farrell stubbed out her cigarette with satisfaction.

If it was a matter of Robbie's welfare, Caitlin was thinking confusedly . . .

'I'll see my young man now, if I may. And thanks for the tea, darling.' Miss Farrell stood up. 'Until tonight, then,' she said.

Caitlin thought sadly of the gentle, unaffected folk she had left behind her in Ireland. She did not know why she should have caught a sudden attack of homesickness, but she had. She put on her beret, noticing that her hair needed washing and her complexion was poor. Why did I agree to meet that woman tonight? she thought.

She wandered off the Unit, suddenly not even as keen as she had been an hour before for the fresh air and the street. Outside she gazed unseeingly at the by now familiar shop fronts and thought of her home town and the shopping of her childhood. The shops had been modest enough: the little haberdasher with her name labels to order, the fishmonger and the general stores which sold everything from buttons to beans.

It all seemed so innocent, so far away from this great city with its intrigues, its fine shops and its cathedrals. Once she had thought that folk were the same the whole world over, but now she wondered. She had belonged in Dublin. And so had he. How had they both arrived at this point together, in the midst of such confusion?

She shut the door of forty-two Cathcart Street

behind her, glad to be in off the street again, and once in her room tried to think clearly about the date she had made with Penelope Farrell. Professionally she had put herself on delicate ground accepting it.

Meeting Miss Farrell outside the hospital meant she must not be drawn into discussion of Robbie's medical or nursing care. All that she could offer his mother would be personal advice and help in accepting his diagnosis. Any detailed discussion of his case should, for ethical reasons, take place only on the Unit.

She was a fool to have agreed to meet the woman, she thought as she prepared supper for herself. Then she bathed and washed her hair, more for her self-confidence than out of vanity, and dressed in navy cord trousers and her guernsey sweater. At the last minute, she knotted a brilliantly coloured silk scarf around her neck, slipped into her boots and fur coat and left the house again.

She enjoyed the walk down Cathcart Street. At least her homesickness seemed to have been banished in the worry over the meeting with Miss Farrell, and that seemed only fair as it was she who had caused it in the first place. The old gaslights cast their soft glow down the street, giving the impression of timelessness and solidity.

It wasn't until she reached Princes Street that Caitlin realised she had mixed up the two big hotels that stood at either end of the street. She found she had to get to the other end and it was already five to eight.

Caitlin crossed to the side which had no shops and counted lampposts to encourage herself in the long walk. She arrived at the British Caledonian Hotel just after eight, breathless and far too hot.

Once through the revolving front doors, she knew she shouldn't have come. She had a sudden impulse to turn round and leave again, but it was too late. An elderly porter had come forward to meet her and ask her her business.

'I want to see a Miss Farrell . . .'

'Ah, yes, madam, Miss Farrell is in the bar. This way, if you please.'

And Caitlin was ushered through the red-carpeted, crystal-chandeliered foyer towards an equally plush bar. She looked in and was horrified. The bar was full of people in full evening regalia, and it was hard to see how she could possibly make anything but a ridiculous entry in her casual gear.

The women were all glittering in sequins, pearls, diamonds and silver clasps over the plain white dresses. The men wore either full evening dress or dinner jacket and bow tie or else they were attired in the kilt appropriate to their clan. Caitlin had never fully understood the significance of the kilt as a battle dress, but now she saw how it accentuated the breadth of shoulders and athleticism of hips, and how daunting were the daggers at the shins.

Staring in, she soon realised that her gaze was being returned by several of the occupants of the bar, and she decided she might as well brave it and walk straight in. She did so, running the gauntlet of a hundred or so pairs of eyes, and silently cursing her own stupidity the while.

Needless to say, Penelope Farrell did not look in the slightest out of place. She was decked out in a sort of purple satin harem suit, which Caitlin admitted looked wonderful on her, and she was superbly relaxed.

'Can I get you a drink, darling?' she asked. 'You look frightfully hot!'

Caitlin sat down heavily, grateful at least for the relative privacy of the corner of the bar in which to blush.

'Thanks, I'd like a large soda water,' she said.

Sipping the cool drink, she began to calm down a little, although Miss Farrell's obvious amusement at her flustered state annoyed her considerably. The other woman was apparently greatly relishing her quiet satin superiority. Caitlin decided to hear her out, then leave, as fast as she could.

She wasn't kept in suspense much longer.

'It's about Robbie, nurse . . .' Miss Farrell stopped short and covered her mouth with her hand in mock horror. 'Oh, I shouldn't call you that in here, should I? What should I call you?'

'My name's Caitlin O'Connell,' Caitlin responded stiffly. She wished Miss Farrell would get on with it.

'What a pretty name! Well, Caitlin, I know I can rely on you to understand my position. It's a very difficult one, you know. I'm going to have to take you into my confidence and trust you completely . . .'

She allowed the waiter to replace her empty whisky glass with a new full one.

' . . . thanks, James. As I was saying, I'll have to tell you simply everthing and place all my trust in you . . .'

It was amazing that Miss Farrell could be even more garrulous here than she usually was on the Unit, but perhaps that was to do with the whisky, Caitlin thought. She waited as patiently and politely as she could for the woman to continue what she was saying. Miss Farrell paused significantly, as she might before delivering an important line.

'It's that dreadful man English,' she pronounced distinctly, 'he's trying to take Robbie away from me.'

Caitlin gasped.

'Well, you needn't look so surprised,' Miss Farrell said in hurt tones, 'if you knew what I'd suffered all these years. And now I've got my baby back again, and nobody's going to take him away from me . . .'

'I'm afraid I don't quite understand you, Miss Farrell,' Caitlin began. But Miss Farrell had not finished yet.

'That man! He's very clever at getting round everybody! I know everyone thinks he's wonderful, but I
tell you he's trying to turn my son against me and
there's nothing I can do. Won't you help me, nurse?
Robbie trusts you. Couldn't you tell the Professor that
he wants to come back to me? He does, you know.
I'll go to the courts. I don't care what it costs. I'd do
anything . . .'

'Miss Farrell,' said Caitlin, shocked, 'this has nothing
whatsoever to do with me. I couldn't possibly do what
you ask, even if . . . You don't seem to understand
my position.'

Miss Farrell's speech had confirmed her in her worst
fears. She would stand up and leave in a moment, as
soon as she had braced herself for the return trip
though the bar.

Then she became aware that the bar was, in fact,
slowly and noisily emptying. She turned round in time
to see Jonathan English appear in the doorway amidst
the last of the departing diners.

Miss Farrell followed her gaze, panic etching itself
on to her features. Caitlin realised that Penelope had
not reckoned on this joint encounter, but there was
little time for speculation.

Jonathan strode over towards their table and
remained standing beside it, fury in his face.

'Ah, Jonathan!' purred Miss Farrell, half rising
from her seat, 'but I wasn't expecting you,' her voice
dropped and she glanced furtively at Caitlin, 'so soon.'

She resumed her seat gracefully and smiled meltingly
at the physician, patting the place beside her on the
velvet upholstery. 'Won't you sit down?'

But Jonathan was preoccupied with Caitlin.

'What are you doing here?' he demanded in a low
voice.

'I . . . Miss Farrell . . . I mean . . . I agreed to
meet Miss Farrell here tonight. I . . . ' She tried

frantically to think why she had agreed to meet the woman at all.

'Go home,' he ordered her. 'Please. Now!'

Caitlin stood up abruptly and snatched her shoulder-bag off the back of her chair. She realised with irritation that the waiter had removed her coat and hung it up somewhere, she did not know where. In an agony of embarrassment she made her way blindly to the door and found her coat hanging solitarily on a stand nearby. She grabbed it, pulled it over her shoulders and fled.

CHAPTER NINE

'I THINK this belongs to you . . .'

Caitlin stopped in her tracks. Breathless, her heart hammering in her chest, she leaned against the railings that closed the darkened park off from Princes Street, and turned and faced the man.

Jonathan caught the pale frightened oval of her face in perfect detail, silhouetted against the massive black bulk of the Castle rock. What had he been doing all these years, he agonised, these ten long years since he had first seen that face?

The fog of confused emotions that had clouded his mind these past few weeks cleared suddenly and gave him a perfect glimpse of all that he had lost.

He thought of the woman now waiting for him back in the hotel, and a terrible molten fury filled him. It had taken him exactly three minutes—since he had banished Caitlin from the bar—to realise the game that Penelope was playing.

It was two weeks since he had rejected her proposal of marriage in the pub at Easter Howgate, and now he knew that she would go to any lengths to get her way by other means. Even to the extent of enlisting the help of Robbie's favourite nurse. If she could not have them both, she'd take the boy . . .

Caitlin still clutched the railings behind her back. But she was calmer. She saw he had her silk scarf; she had untwined it from her neck on her arrival in the hot, sticky bar and put it on the back of her chair. It must have fallen to the floor.

She was reaching out for it, formulating the words

to thank him with, when he took her in his arms. He held her so fast to him that she could not move. Slowly, feeling she did not resist him, Jonathan relaxed. He was trembling himself, afraid of the passion he knew lay just beneath the surface of his longing for her.

Caitlin waited for his next move, numb with the shock his closeness had sent through her. She wanted him never to stir again, but for them to remain bound together like the Castle and its rock from now until time immemorial.

But he stood back from her, and she shivered in the void that took the place of their embrace. He pushed her silk scarf into her hand and met her eyes at last, half ashamed, half desperate.

'I need you . . . to be strong,' he whispered, almost angrily.

She frowned, waiting in confusion for him to finish his sentence. But he was done with her. He turned and was gone. Caitlin watched him walk briskly back towards the hotel and Penelope Farrell, uncertainty and desolation in her heart.

Angus Dougan answered her timid tap on Marian's door. She had remembered the Burns Night supper only as she unlocked the door to forty-two Cathcart Street. It would do as a distraction, she'd thought. Perhaps it was as well to have something to think about, people to talk to, Marian's smile.

'Hello there! Where have you been? We've waited supper for you and the haggis is about bursting to clamber on to the plates!'

Angus put his arm around Caitlin's shoulders and pulled her into the room. There was a real party in progress. Marian had moved her divan bed into the corner of the large room and set trestle tables for twelve or so people down the centre. People stood about with glasses in their hands, and chatter and laughter filled the room.

'Caitlin!' Marian greeted her. 'We wondered where on earth you were! Angus said you were on early. Where have you been?'

'Oh, I just had to meet somebody. Nothing much,' Caitlin said as lightly as she could. 'Sorry I'm late, Marian. I didn't know when it was starting.'

'You didn't know when? *I* didn't know it was on at all!' laughed Marian. 'That rogue Dougan organised it all behind my back. Overflow from the residency booze-up, that's all it is. Because he knows I've always got a bottle of malt in my sideboard. Look at them all—parasites, the lot of them! It's enough to make me ashamed of my profession in advance!'

Sure enough, Marian's treasured Highland single malt whisky sat forlornly on the table almost empty. Uncapped and ravaged, it looked sadly undignified beside the several bottles of lesser brew which had arrived with the guests.

'Come and give me a hand with the haggis, there's an angel,' Marian begged. 'I've been worried to death about it and I'm sure it's overcooked.'

'Not as worried as I've been about eating it, I bet,' Caitlin replied, following her friend into the tiny kitchenette.

'Haven't you ever had it before?' Marian asked. 'It's perfectly delicious! Sheep's innards minced with suet, onions and oatmeal, all seasoned to perfection and boiled in the beastie's stomach! Based on an old French recipe, I believe.'

Caitlin stared at Marian in blatant disbelief.

'Really? Is it really?'

Marian laughed again and lifted the lid off a huge pan of boiling water. Caitlin peeped in and gazed as wide-eyed as the escaping steam would allow at the three large pale plump things that bobbed and rolled within.

'Ugh!' she shuddered.

'Wait until you taste!'

Marian shoved a potato masher into her hand and threw a pack of butter on to the table in front of her. Then she drained two other massive pans and placed one of potato and one of a golden vegetable also on the table.

'Tatties and neeps,' she said.

'Neeps?'

'Turnips!' Marian elucidated. 'Get mashing.'

Caitlin obediently did so, and soon had two creamy mixtures, one golden, one marigold. Meanwhile, Marian had dished the haggis and cut them open, and a truly gorgeous aroma rose from them. Caitlin began to feel hungry again and did a quick calculation of how much she could eat.

' "Fair fa' your honest sonsie face,

Great chieftain o' the puddin' race!" ' quoted Angus to applause as they made a ceremonial entry with the haggis.

Whisky was poured for everybody, the traditional accompaniment to this dish, apparently, and Caitlin regretted having to forfeit hers for a taste of the supper. Half an hour ago she had felt quite capable of matching Miss Farrell's capability for swallowing Scotch. But the new company had done a good job on erasing her memory and Caitlin no longer felt so fraught.

She took a forkful of haggis with some reservation and tasted it. It was a surprise to find it was both savoury and as delicious as Marian had promised. Everybody ate with relish, and soon the feasting gave way to hilarity as people downed their whisky and had their glasses replenished while they quoted and misquoted their national poet.

' "But pleasures are like poppies spread—
You seize the flower, its bloom is shed;
Or like the snowfall in the river,
A moment white—then melts forever." '

Angus was looking fixedly at her while he quoted.
She turned away in the silence, realising that people
had followed his eyes to her face. She knew what he
was saying. She knew he was disappointed in her.
Perhaps Marian had been right and he had really been
serious about her. But what then?

Sooner or later, she knew, she was going to have to
come clean with Angus. She could not keep him
hanging on any longer like this. She would have to
tell him in so many words how she felt—or rather,
how she did not feel about him. And suddenly she
knew it had better be sooner than later.

As Angus drew the ghostly tale of Tam o'Shanter
to a close, so Caitlin closed the chapter of her life
which contained him. She could still feel Jonathan's
arms around her, and they seemed to protect her from
everything: from Burns' queen of witches pursuing
Tam's good mare Meg, from all false feeling and from
Angus.

From Angus, with his handsome face, his blustering
good humour and his whisky-scented kisses. She knew
he wanted her. She knew that one day she could
marry him. But she also knew finally and for certain
that she never would.

'Hey, Caitlin! Let me introduce you two at last.'

Marian led her lanky architect friend over towards
where she stood.

'Hi!' he greeted Caitlin. 'You must keep unearthly
hours—I never see you.'

'I nurse, up at the RCH,' she explained with a smile.

'Ah! Another worker at the Gothic hive!'

'I suppose it is,' returned Caitlin, amused at this

description of the turreted grandeur of her new hospital.

For an incongruous moment she envied Marian this tall, fair-haired, bespectacled student and thought his view of the world probably made for a refreshing change from the world of medicine. Which reminded her of her decision regarding Angus.

She found him in deep discussion with an auburn man whom Caitlin recognised as his counterpart on the Renal Unit. Caitlin hovered nearby, but Angus did not appear to notice her and was in mid-sentence.

'. . . anyway, the old man took him off the case,' she overheard him saying. 'Very difficult position to find himself in, poor so-and-so. Talk about your past catching up with you!' he gave the Renal Unit SHO a heavenward glance. 'And she's a right bitch too, I can tell you.'

Caitlin made for the door. The room was suddenly too hot and crowded for her to breathe. She felt as though she was suffocating. A hand on her arm arrested her.

'Hey, where do you think you're going? I didn't mean to neglect you. I was just talking shop with Harry for a minute . . .'

'That's all right, really, Angus,' Caitlin said quickly. 'I'm just tired. I thought I'd get to bed early for a change.'

'And go off without even saying goodnight? Really, Caitlin!' he sounded injured.

She allowed herself to be drawn into the middle of the floor and into Angus's embrace. He held her close to him, breathing heavily into her hair. Caitlin struggled to find the words she needed to end their affair. Nothing was worse than this enclosure in his arms, which was tightening.

'Caitlin,' he said thickly into her ear, 'you know how I feel about you. I'm not fooling around with you—I'm serious. I've never felt like this before.'

She could feel his chest muscles tense against her, and she pushed herself free of him.

'Angus, I have to talk to you,' she said. 'This can't go on.'

'What can't go on? What do you mean?' Angus frowned, annoyance and puzzlement both evident in his face.

She drew him into an empty corner.

'I can't give you what you want from me, Angus,' she replied simply. 'I'm sorry, Angus, but I don't think we should go on seeing one another off the Unit.'

He turned away from her brusquely and she let herself out of the room, her heart pounding painfully.

But it was not Angus over whom she agonised once downstairs again. She turned the fire on full in her chilly room and knelt before it on the rug in her habitual thinking position. When she got too hot she sat back, her legs curled beneath her, still staring into the flickering flames until her eyes burned.

So. Penelope Farrell belonged to Jonathan's past as well as to his present! That would explain a great deal about the last few hours and days. She recalled with painful clarity their initial meeting in A & E.

She remembered the flash of recognition in Jonathan's face. And then she thought of his embrace and her heart stopped. He was with Penelope now, and perhaps he would always be with her.

Caitlin tried to think about Robbie instead, but she returned to his arms. She could not imagine what had made Jonathan hold her like that, but it was Penelope who held his lasting attention. It was she whom he met, she whose eyes held his across tables, she whom he followed.

And she was deceiving him. Why had Penelope told her that Robbie was being turned against her? How could she be so treacherous behind Jonathan's back? It was more than Caitlin could bear.

And Robbie himself. He could not be turned into her plaything, a pawn in Penelope's game—whatever that was. Robbie needed love and care and a good home. More than anything he needed to feel safe. He might appear as rude and rebellious as any other teenager, but Caitlin knew the struggle he waged privately against his diabetes.

She had always made a special point of conveying Mrs Rae's messages to her adopted son. Robbie received them with a stubborn sullen smile, but Caitlin had tried to go on telling him that he had a home on Skye, where he was loved and cherished for who he was.

She had endlessly reinforced his trust in Jonathan, even though sometimes it had seemed as though she worked hand in glove with him against his will. But it was not by her design that Robbie had chosen her and him.

The boy had singled her out from among the nursing staff for his special trust, just as he had chosen Jonathan from amongst the doctors. And if a patient chose one in whom to confide his fears and hopes it was one's professional duty to respond, to encourage and respect that choice. Nobody knew that better than she did. Nobody knew better the value of such a therapeutic relationship—nobody perhaps but Jonathan English.

No. Whatever was going on between Jonathan and Penelope Farrell, his relationship with Robbie Rae should not have been affected. But it was affected. The consultant had been taken off Robbie's case. Why, why, why?

Caitlin's heart and mind ached simultaneously. She

took her weight off her right arm and squeezed the fingers open and shut to return the circulation. What could she do? She had lost track of time and did not hear the door to her room softly opening.

'Caitlin? Are you there?'

She stood up quickly and put the side light on. She had been sitting in darkness, she realised. Marian crept in and joined her in front of the fire.

'You're in a funny mood tonight,' she said. 'Where did you get to? I missed you upstairs. Are you okay?'

'I think so,' Caitlin replied. 'I'm sorry, Marian. It was no reflection on the party.'

'You left Angus in a sorry state, anyway. Have you two had a fight? He's drinking like a fish and won't speak to a soul. Last I saw of him just now, he was dancing with Joan Hammond, one of my classmates, with about as much pleasure as if she was one of Burns' warlocks.'

'I've finished with him,' Caitlin stated.

'Have you really, Caitlin? But I thought you two were fine earlier.'

'Not really.'

'Caitlin! Something else is the matter. What is it? Tell your aunt Marian! I'm not going back upstairs until you do!' Marian was adamant.

'It's . . . it's nothing, really.' Caitlin played for time. 'I'm a bit worried, that's all, about a patient.'

'A patient?' Marian looked unconvinced. 'It's more than that. Is it to do with that meeting you went to earlier this evening?'

Caitlin sighed.

'I can't tell you, Marian, because I'm so confused myself. It is to do with the person I met this evening, but . . . As soon as I've sorted things out I'd love to talk to you. Honestly, there's nothing I'd like better, but just now, I'm so . . . . confused myself.'

Marian frowned.

'Okay. But wouldn't you like to come back upstairs for half an hour? Take your mind off things for a bit? Oh, God, Angus! I suppose he's the last person you want to see? Listen, I'll pop back down again later, after everybody's gone. We can talk then.'

Caitlin went to the door with Marian, then suddenly stopped her in her tracks.

'Marian, why should a senior medical man suddenly be taken off a case?'

Marian looked bemused, then thought hard for a moment.

'Funnily enough, we had a talk about that not so long ago, from some lawyer fellow: "Ethical considerations in patient care", or some such pompous title, it had. I can't for the life of me remember what he said. Just a minute.' Marian paused, a perplexed frown on her face. 'It's very unusual,' she mused.

'What is?'

'For someone to be taken off a case.'

Time seemed to stand still until Marian spoke again.

'It's when there's emotional involvement between the doctor and the patient,' she said at last. 'That's about the only indication. When there's family ties or something like that, something that could effect the doctor's professional judgment. Why do you ask?'

Caitlin swallowed hard.

'Oh, no reason really,' she said as lightly as she could, while Marian stared uncomprehendingly at her, 'it was just something I was wondering about.'

'Well, don't wonder too hard or too long. You're very overwrought tonight, Caitlin. I'm worried about you.'

Caitlin closed the door gently behind her friend.

'Emotional involvement between the doctor and the patient', the words echoed around inside her head like those of a cathedral choir. 'Family ties', of course! Of course. In an agony of self-reproach, she wondered how she could have been so blind, so stupid.

'Something that could affect the doctor's professional judgment', Marian had said. A thousand things paraded themselves through Caitlin's mind: one incident after another waited to be understood in the light of this new knowledge, and she went through them all.

She remembered Robbie's admission, the letter he'd written to 'Dr Sassenach', the rescue in the Pentlands. It all made sense now. Everything fell into place. One by one the pieces of the puzzle clicked into position until the whole picture lay before her, complete in every detail—a picture so complete that it excluded her finally, for ever.

'I need you to be strong'—that was what he had said. She had forgotten that until now. Yes, she would be strong. But how—oh, how? For the first time since she was seventeen she found herself praying devoutly for something that seemed impossible: the strength to carry on.

When Marian came back downstairs two hours later, she found Caitlin sound asleep, fully dressed on her bed. And the wing of dark hair that fell across her cheek was still wet with tears.

Marian remembered that Caitlin was off next day and came down to share breakfast. She had a confession to make.

She found Caitlin already up, bathed and dressed in jeans and a lovely peach-coloured mohair sweater that complemented her colouring beautifully and distracted from the dark shadows under her grey eyes. Marian decided not to allude to last night in case she should upset Caitlin again. There was no point in that. And anyway, she had other business on her mind.

'Caitlin,' she began the moment their breakfast was over, 'are you really quite sure about Angus?' She blushed. 'I mean, it is really over between you two?'

Caitlin looked taken aback.

'Yes, I hope so,' she said. 'As far as I'm concerned it's over. Why?'

'Well, it's just that I . . . I mean, we . . . I mean, Angus and I sort of . . . got together last night,' Marian managed finally.

'You and Angus!' Caitlin exclaimed. 'But what about your architect? He was there last night. I thought . . .'

Marian looked somewhat shamefaced.

'We medics,' she said, 'like to stick together in the end, It sounds awful, I know. But Angus was so miserable and he sort of came and cried on my shoulder and I felt so sorry for him. I hope you don't mind, Caitlin? I hope it's really true that you don't want to see him any more?'

Caitlin felt sorry for her; she was so obviously conscience-stricken.

'It is true, Marian,' she said. 'You mustn't worry about it, honestly.' She began to feel like giggling. 'I hope you're both . . .' her nose twitched, 'very happy together!'

Marian joined her in fits of uncontrollable giggles.

'I feel really stupid,' she said after a minute, 'after all that "just good friends" stuff I gave you about Angus and me.'

'Oh, well,' Caitlin responded, 'that should have told me straight away. All the best people from Royalty down use that one.'

'The funny thing is,' said Marian thoughtfully, 'that's exactly what we always have been—just good friends, I mean—until now.' She blushed again.

Caitlin made a second cup of coffee while she decided she really was pleased about Marian and

Angus and didn't regret her decision of last night. It all seemed to be far away, in another reality.

She handed Marian her new cup of coffee.

'No lectures today?' she asked.

'No. Angus and I thought we'd take the day out somewhere. He's off today too . . . as you probably know. We thought we'd go off somewhere in the car,' said Marian with a shy smile and a shrug, 'a sort of celebration, or something.'

Caitlin sipped her coffee contemplatively, then gave Marian a quick smile.

'I see!' she said.

'And I wondered what your plans were for the day, actually . . .'

Surely Marian wasn't going to ask her along?

'It was really freezing when I went out to get the bread rolls and milk for breakfast. Siberian! Not a day for outings, really.'

Caitlin mused on her friend's words. They seemed at odds with her previous ones, but maybe that was just her own poor concentration this morning. As for herself, she hadn't given today a thought yet. She didn't have any plans at all.

'I don't know what I'm doing,' she said. 'Why?'

'So you won't be needing your fur coat?' Marian ventured.

'So that's it!' exclaimed Caitlin.

'No, really, Caitlin. If you've any plans to go out, I wouldn't dream . . . I just thought, after last night, you might be planning a quiet day in . . . I . . .' Marian gazed sheepishly at her.

'You can take it,' said Caitlin in Penelope Farrell mode. 'Take my coat, my friendship, my man . . .' she gestured tragically, 'take it all!'

'Oh, Caitlin, don't!' protested Marian, horrified. 'That sounds really awful.'

'Very well, then,' Caitlin adopted her natural style.

'You're welcome to them—all three!'

She slipped the coat out of her cupboard and on to Marian's shoulders.

'I have to say, it looks lovely on you, modom,' she said. 'But he'll recognise it,' she added cheekily.

The house felt terribly empty after the door had clicked closed behind Marian and Angus. Caitlin hadn't actually seen him, but she'd heard his voice, and the warmth and intimacy in it as he passed some trivial comment to Marian stopped her heart for an instant before she reminded herself of his unwanted embrace.

She sat in front of the fire, hugging her knees, wondering what to do with the great expanse of day that lay before her. She could read. And she had been meaning to join the library. That would be a pleasant way to spend a couple of hours. Yet it did not really appeal; nothing she thought of did.

She began to tidy her room, clearing away the breakfast things and making everything look pretty and in place. The task was too soon done, and she was staring out at the northern sky envying the seagulls. That was what she would do! She would go back to Cramond.

She put another thin jersey on beneath her mohair and her anorak and hoped she would be warm enough if she stayed in the sunshine. Outside it was bitterly cold, but the sky was clear and bright. It was good to board a bus and leave the city centre behind, with all its memories.

She tried not to think of Marian and Angus, perhaps on the road to Killin. She banished all the members of the nursing and medical staff of the Unit, the patients and their relatives, and set her face steadily for the Firth of Forth.

What did she want from life? She evidently did not
want a relationship with an eligible young medical
colleague. She knew she did not want fleeting affairs.
She did not want parties and Peter Pan excitement,
and yet she could not imagine settling down. She did
not think she would ever have children now. How
could she?

She had faced up to that one recently. How could
she inflict the same suffering on her own child as she
had suffered, as Robbie Rae was suffering now? Only
under the most extraordinary circumstances could she
ever contemplate such a thing; only with the support
of a man who knew exactly what was entailed . . .
She stopped thinking.

The open horizon of the sea spread before her.
What did she want? It was no use feeling lonely now.
She had to build from here alone. She would ask
Sister Fairfield about the clinical nurse specialist job.
For too long she had been avoiding discussing it with
her and pretending not to hear her hints that she
should be involved in some kind of pilot study on the
scheme.

She would have to consider the question carefully
and put herself forward for the post if she wanted it.
Virginia Fairfield was nowhere near retirement and
Janet Harrison was in line for her job if and when she
did resign for some reason. It was time for serious
planning, Caitlin told herself.

She wandered out a way along the line of stones
which led to the lighthouse, but it reminded her of
someone. She turned briskly back, the wind pushing
at her, urging her towards the river. From here, the
village of white cottages seemed to be painted along
the shore. Seagulls sat motionless, their feathers ruffled
by the wind, all along the pier, and the sea spread all
around as if frozen.

She pushed her hands deep into her anorak pockets

and thought once more of Marian. It was ironical that she could so easily be sitting now where Marian sat, beside Angus, in the same fur coat. She smiled into the bitter wind. How strange were the ways of the world! She gained the mainland and made for the river.

The ferryman was silent and dour and just as suspicious as if he had never seen Caitlin before. He took her money and punted her across the narrow water without comment. Once on the path, sheltered by scrub and sand dunes from the worst of the sea wind, she began to enjoy her excursion. She forgot work and worries and walked happily along.

Suddenly feeling that she was being watched, she turned and saw beside the path a little white furry animal. It had stopped in some impressions in the sand: footprints too small for an adult foot. It stood up in one of them, tall and slender on its hind legs, and peered at Caitlin curiously. She returned its gaze with amusement, amazed that it showed no fear of her.

It held its front paws up in front while its small intelligent face, crowned by rounded ears with tufts of fur, searched hers. After a few moments of this, it disappeared completely down an almost invisible hole, and Caitlin expected that was the last she would see of it.

But a second or two later it popped up again, not out of the same hole, but nearby, and sat up again, eyeing her as if to see her reaction. She smiled. It disappeared again, and came up again almost at her feet.

Fascinated, Caitlin watched the game for quite some time. She decided he was a stoat. She had heard an uncle who lived in the country describe exactly this behaviour and at the time she had not really believed him. It sounded so incredible that a wild animal should play with a human being like this. She felt honoured to witness it for herself.

The game completely distracted her from the initial interest in the footprints, so that by the time she took to the path again she had forgotten them. The woods were lovely today, tall and solemn in their winter sleep, yet glistening with moisture as the sun melted the frost which had coated their branches.

She came to the fork in the path and automatically took the one that led to her secret cove. The path wound round and down until the small crescent of pebbly beach shore came in sight.

Robbie saw her first. He scrambled away behind a high rocky outcrop and tried to hide. But he was too late; Caitlin had seen his small figure darting for cover as surely as the little wild thing had just done. She walked slowly and quietly over the strand, her boots hardly disturbing the pebbles, and peeped round the edge of the rock.

'Robbie!'

He stared at her with startled golden-brown eyes.

'Robbie! What are you doing here?' Caitlin crouched down beside the huddled figure of the boy.

'We went for a walk,' he said bravely enough.

'You what? You and who?'

'Me an' Jamie.'

Caitlin shivered involuntarily, more with anxiety than with cold.

'And who said you could leave the hospital, Robbie?' she enquired gently.

'Nurse Adrian,' Robbie said without hesitation. 'She said you said we could go.'

'I?' Caitlin repeated with horror.

'That's what she said.'

She thought rapidly. She knew that Nurse Adrian was in charge of the Unit this morning—her last—and that Sister was on late. She had made up the off-duty rota herself earlier in the week and could recall exactly what she and Sister had said about Nurse Adrian's farewell tea party on the Unit and what shift she should work.

'George McLeod was away out for a wee stroll himself and she said we could go along too,' Robbie continued.

Mr McLeod, the haemophiliac, was due for discharge and came and went from the Unit much as he liked these days. Caitlin fought the fury she felt for Nurse Adrian.

'Robbie, I'm going to take you back to the hospital now,' she said quietly.

She expected him to argue, or for some show of resentment from him. But there was nothing of the sort. He took her hand meekly.

'I like it here,' he said. 'It's a wee bit like Skye.'

'How do you feel, Robbie? Have you had anything to eat?'

'I'm no' too bad, but I don't feel that great . . .'

Suddenly he was no longer full of the bravado which had taken him out of the hospital and brought him here. Suddenly he was just a frightened child sobbing in her arms.

'It's all right, Robbie. You'll be okay, don't worry. We'll soon be back, and nobody will blame you.'

'I don't want to stay in the hospital, Nurse O'Con,' he mumbled into her sleeve. 'I want hame.'

'Did you say home, Robbie?' she asked softly.

'Aye.' The boy wiped his nose and eyes savagely on his own sleeve. 'I want hame to Skye,' he told her. 'Have you seen my ma?' he wanted to know. 'She knows a' aboot my diabetes—the jags and a' that. I'll be a' right at hame wi' her. I want to see her, Nurse O'Con. Will you write her for me, an' tell her to pick me up?'

'Yes, Robbie, I'll tell her.'

Caitlin tightened her hold on Robbie's hand.

'Jamie went to the picture house to see a film,' he told her as they walked up through the deserted village to the main road, 'but I wanted a wee bit thinking time, so I cam' down here, like you.'

'I should never have told you about the cove,' Caitlin breathed, quickening her pace. 'It would have been all my fault if . . .'

At least Jamie would be relatively easy to find. She had been crazy to tell Robbie about Cramond; she knew how impressionable he was. She would have to confess to Sister Fairfield.

Her mind full of worry about when a bus would come, whether Robbie would be all right during the journey, how he had come to be here at all, she had almost forgotten the joy she had felt when he had said he wanted to go home.

'I wanted to think over what's happened to me,' he said now. 'I've decided it's no good pretending that there's nothing the matter with me an' I'm no' sick. I'll just need to get used to the idea and get on wi' it as best I can.'

Caitlin hugged him, and was glad of the excuse to look out for the bus to hide her tears. When it came she found a seat quickly. Robbie rested his head listlessly against her shoulder. It was well past both their lunchtimes; she had planned to get something locally at midday. She willed the bus on, and when it at last reached Princes Street helped Robbie out and hailed a passing taxi.

Within a few minutes they were deposited at the entrance to A & E by an experienced cab driver.

'I knew you was a nurse, hen, the minute you said "RCH",' he told her as she paid him. 'What with the laddie no' too grand. Thanks, hen, and God bless you!'

Sister Everton was standing in the door of her office

just inside A & E when Caitlin made a rather embarrassing entry with Robbie trailing miserably at her side.

'Ah!' said Sister, 'Staff Nurse O'Connell, isn't it? And what have we here? An absconder?'

She shook her head disapprovingly, while Caitlin wondered anew at her psychic powers.

'Yes, Sister. We were just on our way back up to the UYCS, Sister.'

'It's our young diabetic, isn't it? Looking a wee bit peely-wally, eh? Away upstairs, laddie, and get something in that belly of yours!'

Robbie looked distinctly frightened. Caitlin gave Sister Everton a nervous smile.

'Thanks, Sister. I'm sorry to walk in through the department, but the taxi-man . . .'

'Och, save your breath to cool your porridge, Staff! Off you get, lassie. Take a wheelchair—the lad can scarcely walk straight!'

Caitlin did as she was bid, feeling exactly like a reprimanded schoolgirl. That was who Sister Everton reminded her of—she must tell Mary in her next letter—Mother Superior at their old convent school. She recognised the same old mingled trust and trepidation in her own response.

Robbie looked very small and frail in the wheelchair, but he felt too weak-kneed to refuse it. Caitlin took him up in the lift and pushed him in through the Unit doors. The reception that awaited them there proved more daunting even than Sister Everton had been.

CHAPTER TEN

PENELOPE Farrell dominated the scene. Clad from head to toe in scarlet, she cast her eyes from Sister Fairfield to Professor Carstairs and back again as though neither they nor heaven could help her.

It took all three a moment or two to recognise the occupant of the wheelchair, and Caitlin, in mufti. Then Sister, who had obviously only just arrived on duty, took charge of the situation.

'Into the side room, please, Staff Nurse. I think you'll find Robbie's lunch still waiting for him there. And if you'd just check his general observations and find a specimen of urine, I'll be in right away . . .'

But Miss Farrell could remain in the background no longer. She rushed up to the wheelchair and pulled Robbie to his feet and into her embrace.

Robbie just stood there motionless in her arms, a blank expression on his face. It was some time before the woman realised that he was not responding to her. Then she held him away from her at arm's length, fury in her eyes.

'Robbie! How could you do this wicked thing to us? I've been so frantic. You naughty, selfish boy! What am I to do with you?'

The boy stared into space.

'Nothing,' he answered.

'Nothing! Is that all you've got to say? After all you've put me through?'

'That's all I've got to say to you,' Robbie replied.

He made off unsteadily towards his room. Caitlin caught him up and took his arm. They were still well within earshot when Miss Farrell proceeded to bemoan her fate.

'Oh, my goodness. Oh, I don't know what I'm to do. I feel quite faint!'

She still had quite a substantial audience in Sister and Professor Carstairs.

'I should calm down a wee bit, m'dear,' the Professor suggested laconically. 'I'm sure it can't be as bad as all that. The boy's back, and that's the most important thing, now isn't it?'

And with that he disappeared into the doctors' room, much to Miss Farrell's rage.

Sister Fairfield appraised the woman coldly. She resorted to the age-old answer to distressed relatives, although she was not sure that Miss Farrell qualified.

'I'll see if I can find you a cup of tea, Miss Farrell, if you'd just like to step this way.'

A few minutes later Sister appeared in Robbie's room. Caitlin had settled him in his armchair, wrapped warmly in a blanket, and he was slowly and painstakingly eating his lunch. He still looked rather shaky, but there was no hint of rebellion in the air, which was more than could have been said recently about the boy.

'So, Staff, the wanderer returns!' Sister smiled with genuine warmth at them both. 'And where did you find him? No, never mind, you can tell me that later.' She looked at the recordings Caitlin had just charted.

'Well, young Robbie, you seem to be in better shape than you deserve! I hear you took a wee outing wi' your friend and comrade in crime Jamie Ferguson. We've found him too, you'll be pleased to hear, no doubt. He was prudent enough to tell George McLeod how much he admired James Bond, so he was no' too hard to find.'

Robbie smiled weakly and rather apologetically.

'Staff, will you come and have a wee word with me,

please? I'll ask Staff Harrison to come in and make sure this wee rascal eats his lunch.'

'I'm going to eat it all, Sister, honestly,' Robbie promised.

Sister rumpled his hair affectionately. 'Oh, aye!' she said.

When they were in the cloakroom—the only free staff space left available to them—she turned to Caitlin.

'So. This is a fine carry-on. On your day off, too, Staff O'Connell!'

'It's all my fault, Sister,' Caitlin burst out. 'I told him about the cove at Cramond where I found him today. It was ages ago, and I didn't think anything of it at the time. But now I see how stupid I was. I feel so awful . . .'

'Stuff and nonsense, Staff!' Sister interrupted her. 'What on earth are you saying? It was nothing whatso-ever to do with you. Nurse Adrian told me herself that she told the laddies they could go—with your permission.'

Caitlin stared at Sister in astonishment.

'She did?'

'She did indeed. It's time you stopped protecting that girl, Staff Nurse O'Connell, and start looking after yourself. I owe you an apology, come to that.'

Sister smoothed her white dress over her hips in a momentary loss of poise.

'That girl has had a number of problems,' she went on, 'not least of which was that she wanted to staff here after she passed State and I gave the post to you instead.'

Caitlin listened in disbelief.

'I decided not to tell you before now, for various reasons, and so you see, you've been working at a disadvantage with Nurse Adrian ever since you took up your post on the Unit. If anything, it's my fault that this unfortunate incident happened this morning.

It's a pure act of reprisal on her part, and I should have seen it coming.'

'So she really did have a grudge against me . . .' Caitlin murmured.

'Aye, I'm afraid she did. She needs help, and I'll have a word with Sister Duncan on the Renal Unit today and make sure she gets some counselling before she sits State and support for as long as she needs it afterwards. It's a shame for the lass. I should have got her help sooner.'

Sister paused.

'Anyway, I hope now that you're here, you'll join us for her farewell party. It's in my office at two, as we discussed earlier in the week. Two—in half an hour! Good grief, where has the past hour gone?'

'There's one more thing, Sister . . .' Caitlin remembered. 'Robbie wants to see Mrs Rae. He asked me on our way back to the hospital.'

Sister Fairfield gave her a searching look and then a warm smile flooded her features.

'About time too!' she said. 'Would you give her a ring, Staff? I know you're officially off duty, but I'm sure she'd much appreciate it if it was you who called.'

'Should I come up right away, nurse? Or should I wait for the visiting?'

'I'm sure it'd be fine if you came up straight away, Mrs Rae,' said Caitlin, trying to keep her voice steady. It was hard to match Margot Rae for dignity and self-control. 'I'm sure Robbie will be very pleased to see you.'

'Well, thank you, nurse. And I hope I get to see you too, when I'm up.'

Saying goodbye, Caitlin hoped this would be the last, the very last, of those terrible telephone calls.

Nurse Adrian sidled into Sister's room and sat down

as if she was ashamed to be there. Staff Nurse Harrison
and Caitlin were already assembled, along with two
students, one from the early and one from the late
shift. Caitlin wondered what had happened to Penelope
Farrell, and supposed she must have gone off to find
some lunch to sustain herself over her shock.

Sister must have briefed the other staff nurse à
propos Nurse Adrian, for Janet was making a special
effort to be nice to the third year. She handed her a
small gift-wrapped package and watched while she
unwrapped it.

'A pen and pencil set for the top pocket of your
royal blue dress,' Janet told her warmly. The student
nurses swapped their pink uniforms for royal blue
when they passed State final examinations to qualify
as staff nurses.

'Thanks,' Nurse Adrian murmured.

Everybody began to drink their tea and gossip until
the purpose of the get-together seemed forgotten.
Caitlin was just about to slip away when Nurse Adrian
touched her arm.

'I'm sorry, Staff O'Connell,' the girl whispered. 'I
didn't mean anything so bad.'

Caitlin swallowed the lump that had risen to her
throat.

'That's okay, Nurse Adrian. I hope everything goes
okay for you on the Renal Unit. I hope you'll be
happy there.'

'Sister seems nice,' she replied.

'Yes,' Caitlin affirmed, 'I've heard she's really sweet.
I'm sure it'll be a good place to sit State.'

'I hope so.'

'Good luck,' said Caitlin.

'Thanks, Staff O'Connell.'

Caitlin retrieved her jersey and anorak, then realised

that she should tell Sister Fairfield that she was off.
The Unit seemed oddly still, in that mid-afternoon lull
when two shifts of nursing staff overlap, sharing what
little work there was. There was no sign of Sister.

'Hello, nurse. Well, I'm here.'

It was Mrs Rae, a nervous smile on her lips, and a
slight flush of excitement on her cheeks. She gave
Caitlin's outfit a puzzled glance, as if, seeing her in
mufti, she wondered if she was in the right place at
the right time.

'Oh, you just caught me, Mrs Rae. I was just going
off,' said Caitlin. 'I'm sure Sister will want a word
with you. I was just looking for her myself . . .'

Sister emerged at that instant from Robbie's room,
Penelope Farrell in her wake.

'Ah, Mrs Rae! Super!' smiled Sister. 'If you'd like a
word with your sonny, I'll speak to you in just a
moment, my dear.'

Robbie must have heard Sister's words, for he flew
out of his room and into the waiting arms of his
adoptive mother.

'Oh, Ma,' he sobbed, 'oh, Ma, Ma!'

'That's a' right, my bairn, that's a' right,' soothed
Mrs Rae, tears shining in her eyes. 'No harm's done,
my wee one—Mammy's here.'

Caitlin gently moved Mrs Rae's shopping bag out
of the doorway so that she could shut Robbie's door
behind the two. Sister gave Caitlin a significant glance
and then turned her attention to the transfixed
Penelope Farrell.

'Aye, some reunions deserve a wee bit of privacy,'
Sister muttered as if to herself, enraging the other
woman visibly.

'I wish to speak to the Professor,' she demanded.

'Professor Carstairs is lecturing this afternoon,' Sister
told her. 'But if you come back in the morning, I'll
make an appointment for you to see him then.'

'I need to speak to him now,' Miss Farrell declared furiously. 'I can't wait until tomorrow. You don't seem to realise how all this has affected me . . . phoning to ask if the child is with me, when he's under your legal custody while he's in this hospital . . . I could sue; I shall consult my lawyer . . .'

'You may do just as you please, Miss Farrell,' responded Sister coolly, 'and I shall make an appointment for you to see Professor Carstairs in the morning. Will nine-thirty suit you? That should fit in nicely before his wards rounds. Of course, I'll need to check with his secretary that he has no prior engagements . . .'

She swept the other woman along like dust before a broom, and Caitlin followed at a little distance, feeling somewhat sorry for Penelope Farrell. She was a pathetic sight all of a sudden, rejected by her son and victim of her own machinations.

But Caitlin's pity did not last long. They had no sooner reached the doctors' room than the door opened and Jonathan English emerged.

Penelope Farrell threw herself at him, weeping unrestrainedly.

Caitlin did not wait to see his arms close around the woman. She almost ran past them and out of the Unit, Penelope Farrell's choked, barely audible 'Jonathan!' ringing in her ears.

Louder than the bells of St Giles' Cathedral, deeper than the boom of the one o'clock cannon from the Castle battlements, that name resounded through Caitlin: Jonathan! Jonathan!

It followed her remorselessly. In vain she gazed into shop windows on Princes Street. Her own reflection met her stare, hollow-eyed and haunted. In vain she walked her favourite route between the Georgian houses. Today they looked like a giant stage set. Nothing was real. Nothing could comfort her.

He was lost to her completely. They had lost Robbie, but they still had one another, he and that woman. And she had nothing and no one. She wished she was back in Ireland, an innocent girl. She wished he . . . but it was no good. All that was in the past. There was no going back. There was only the empty future.

She thought about leaving Scotland. It would be unendurable to stay here now. And yet she had come to love Edinburgh, this city of spires and aspirations. And there was her work, after all the years of waiting.

The RCH was a wonderful hospital, full of possibilities. She thought of the Unit, of Sister Fairfield's honest, good administration, even of Nurse Adrian. She had rarely met a more caring, imaginative team than the one she had joined a mere month ago. She thought of Angus and Marian; the new generation of doctors. Edinburgh was a wonderful place in which to care for the sick; a place whose luminous present matched its glowing traditions.

She did not want to leave. But how could she stay here near Jonathan? Or—she rephrased the question to herself with brutal honesty—how could she face being near him and Penelope? Even the thought of living in the same city with them was agony to her.

She bought herself a cup of coffee in a basement coffee shop. The place smelled of freshly-ground coffee beans and home-made scones with melting butter, just like her mother used to make.

Caitlin remembered what a scandal had been caused in her home town when her parents had broken up after nearly twenty-five years of marriage. It had been terrible to be at the centre of such a scandal as a teenager, and yet when she thought about it now, how innocent it seemed.

Good-hearted and kindly, the neighbours had been quick to apportion blame, but just as quick to offer sympathy to both parties and to extend hospitality to the children. The memory made Caitlin homesick anew, but she knew she could go back no more as a child to her childhood home.

She had to make a life for herself here, out in the world. She had to forge new ways for herself and build new relationships. That was what she had always promised herself. Looking back, home looked all that she wanted; but when she was there she knew that that was not true.

And the world was full of different hardships from those she had known at home. The problems that she met out here were bigger, less understandable. Yet there was no running away from them, for all that. Next time she went home she would have a new life to show her aunt, her mother and Mary; a life of which she was proud, and a life to which she would want to return.

And what was she doing about building that life? She was sitting here, wistfully dreaming, drinking her black coffee and thinking about Angus and Marian. Angus and Marian, driving back from Killin. Perhaps stopping for a drink . . .

It would not do. Life was passing her by, and she was sitting on the bank watching the river flow past: Robbie and Mrs Rae, Penelope and Jonathan . . .

She got up, paid for her coffee and left the café. To her surprise, the sky was darkening already and soon it would be evening. Well, she had passed the day that had stretched ahead so dauntingly, and that was something. What a terrible waste, at twenty-seven, to pass a whole day and be glad it was gone!

This was where she turned over a new leaf, she vowed. January had been a month of indecision, of changes and of uncertainty. But now it was nearly over and she would begin the new year properly.

She plunged into the narrow darkness of Rose Street, determined to vary her way home, to underline her new resolve. It was not such a good idea. The little street was full of jewellers' shops, and engagement, wedding and eternity rings sparkled at her whichever way she looked. Then she remembered her shamrock silver charm, and her heart turned over.

Nothing had gone right since she'd lost it—nothing. She stopped, wondering where exactly she was. A pub near where she stood opened up and a barman gave her a friendly wink as he propped open the door. She must have looked at him in surprise, because he grinned and nodded at the clock above the bar.

'Been waiting long, hen? It's only just gone five!'

Embarrassed, Caitlin hurried away, emerging into a street which she could take for home. By now it was darkening fast and she realised she was cold.

There had been something she had meant to do today. What was it? She racked her brains. She knew that this morning she had made a mental note, before Marian had appeared for breakfast. What an age ago that seemed now.

Breakfast! It dawned on her that she had not actually had anything to eat since breakfast. She had absentmindedly chewed some biscuits at Nurse Adrian's tea-party and thought she could manage on those until supper time, but now she wondered . . .

And the thing she had forgotten was her insulin. This morning she had noticed she was almost out of the supplies of PZI and Lente insulin she had brought with her from Dublin, and she would not even have enough of the former for the next day. Ever since she had arrived in Edinburgh she had meant to find herself a new G P, but so much had happened since that she had not given it much thought.

And now it was too late. All the family doctors'

surgeries would be closed until evening surgery—even if they had those up here. She'd have to look in the phone book to see if there was one nearby and ask if she could see him this evening, and then find a duty chemist . . .

What was that that Sister Fairfield had said about looking after herself? Caitlin cursed her own stupidity. She would ring the Unit, that was the best idea. Sister would certainly not mind lending her some insulin until the following day, when she could find a doctor. She could pick it up later, when she'd eaten.

She did not feel well. She let herself into number forty-two Cathcart Street and made straight for the public telephone in the hall. The last thing she remembered was picking up the receiver and dialling the number of the RCH. But she must have asked for the Unit before she passed out.

'Caitlin? Caitlin! Wake up, for God's sake!'

Caitlin stirred.

'I'm diabetic,' she murmured from subconscious survival mechanisms, 'glucose.'

'Caitlin—drink this.'

She put her lips to the cup that was offered her and sipped the sweetened orange juice it contained, then lay back and tried to focus the confusion in her mind.

'I didn't eat . . . It was so cold . . .'

'Caitlin, it's okay now. Just rest.'

'I didn't mean him to go . . . she . . . he . . . I told him about the cove. It was so pretty there . . .' she faltered.

'Caitlin, Caitlin!'

Whose was that voice? It was so far away. Yet she felt she could recognise it. It said her name to her before, long ago, in a dream.

Then the glucose began to pulse through her veins,

reviving her, and she could feel her strength returning miraculously to her limbs. She opened her eyes with an immense effort and saw Jonathan English.

He was sitting on the edge of her bed, in her own room. In one hand he held her empty cup, and in the other lay her own hand, pale and cold.

'Caitlin!' he said.

She scrutinised his face, still unable to divide dream from reality. She had dreamed him so often in this room. How could he be here in truth? But his fingers were warmly clasped around her own. She could feel them. And she could see his frown and the clouded depths of his brown eyes.

'Jonathan?' she whispered.

'Yes,' he said, 'I'm here, Caitlin. Thank God I answered the phone, purely by chance. Don't worry, I've brought your insulin. Don't worry . . . about anything.'

'I rang the Unit,' she recalled slowly.

'Yes, Caitlin. You rang the Unit and told me you'd run out of insulin. Oh, Caitlin, what a fool I've been!'

'You . . .?'

'Caitlin, I want to make you some supper, and then I want to talk to you.'

'But I . . .' she struggled up into a sitting position. 'I can do . . .'

'Caitlin, let me do something for you.' Jonathan's voice was low. 'You've done so very much for me.'

She heard him busy in the kitchen, and still she could not make it come true for herself. What had she done for him? What was he doing here? He could have sent an ambulance, anything . . .

He brought her cheese on toast and a glass of milk, and sat silently watching her eat and drink. Then he went over to the window and pulled aside the curtain. She finished her meal while he gazed out over the rooftops towards the sea, his back to her.

Then she put her tray down beside the bed and
swung her feet over the edge. She sat there watching
him while the moon rose and stars began to show in
the dark blue sky.

She thought of all she knew of him, of all the years
she had thought of him and cherished his memory. It
hardly seemed possible that he was standing here now.
Suddenly, she did not want him to turn around and
be another Jonathan; the Jonathan with lines on his
face and hard, dark eyes. The Jonathan who loved
Penelope Farrell.

She held her breath, willing the moment to last for
ever, unchanged. And then she realised he was waiting
for her to speak, to explain herself. He was waiting
for her to tell him how she had known where Robbie
was today, and why . . . She steeled herself and heard
her own voice echoing around the room.

'I underestimated him, you see. Robbie . . .' but
she could not go on.

The figure at the window did not move.

'He's my son,' he said.

Caitlin slid off the bed and ran to him. She put her
arms around him.

'I know, I know,' she repeated softly. 'Jonathan, I
know.'

Gradually he relaxed. His arms went around her
too and they stood locked together. He held her closer
and closer until she felt united with him for ever. Her
face pressed against him, she felt tears of relief, of
pain and of sympathy leave her eyes and dampen his
shirt.

At last he freed her. She looked into his face and
saw that he had been crying too. He took her tenderly
and sat beside her on the bed.

'I knew Penelope Farrell fourteen years ago,' he
began simply. 'When she got pregnant I wanted to
marry her—I thought it was the only thing to do. I

wanted to look after her and the baby.'

He spoke very quietly, very tiredly, as if relating a story which he knew too well by heart. Caitlin listened, watching his face.

'She was just a struggling actress then, working in repertory. She was part of a company who were putting on a revue during the Festival, and I was helping with the lighting backstage. I loved the theatre then. I don't think I do any more.' He looked at her, a sad smile on his lips.

'Penelope was an ambitious young woman, and naturally, a baby wasn't going to get in her way. I was nothing to interest her either, of course,' Jonathan added softly, 'a penniless young medic, if you'll excuse the cliché.'

Caitlin raised her eyebrows. She did not feel like laughing. Suddenly the whole disastrous fiasco with Penelope Farrell made horrible sense.

'And so she had the baby adopted and slept her way to stardom. And that was the last you heard of her or Robbie. Until now, when she thought she'd reclaim her handsome young son and a successful medical consultant husband into the bargain?'

Jonathan grimaced.

'Not a very pretty story, is it?' he asked humbly.

'You have nothing to feel ashamed about. She . . .' Caitlin was too angry to speak.

'I didn't know how to cope when she turned up that day in Casualty with the boy,' Jonathan continued quietly. 'I was so shocked that all sense left me. I simply couldn't respond to you at all, Caitlin. I didn't know what she was doing with him—it was as simple as that. I'd comforted myself with the knowledge that he was being cared for by a loving couple, that he had a good home. Perhaps that he was better off there than with two parents who didn't love one another . . .'

He cleared his throat.

'I've had the devil's own job telling that bloody woman to leave him alone, with his adoptive parents, where he belongs,' he said.

'Poor Jonathan!'

'He doesn't know about me, of course, not . . . about my being . . .' he paused painfully.

' "Dear Dr Sassenach",' murmured Caitlin, taking his hand.

He looked at her for the first time in a long while, his eyes full.

'You were wonderful with him, Caitlin, when I could do nothing.'

'I only gave him what he deserved,' she said.

'And what about what you deserve, Caitlin?'

He took something out of the inside pocket of his jacket and held it out towards her in the palm of his hand.

'Look, Caitlin. I found this the morning that I met you again. It was lying near the bus stop outside the RCH. It reminded me so strongly of you. It was incredible.'

She looked. It was the silver shamrock charm, nestling in a soft coiled pool of silver chain. She caught her breath.

'It was broken,' he continued. 'I had it mended and then kept it, carrying it with me all the time, waiting for the time I'd give it to you . . .'

'But it's mine!' Caitlin exclaimed. 'I lost it that morning, when I paid my bus fare, I think. I was late . . .'

It was Jonathan's turn to be amazed.

'I could feel you in it,' he said slowly. 'I knew I must find you again . . .'

She covered his mouth swiftly with her fingers.

'Sssh! Don't say another word, Jonathan. We'll break the spell.'

He silently and gently clasped the necklace about her neck, then kissed her throat above the tiny shamrock leaf.

'How did you come to be here, in Edinburgh?' she asked. It was the last question she wanted to ask of him. She felt she knew everything else about him now.

He looked thoughtfully into her eyes for a moment, his own darkening before he spoke.

'I've never admitted this to myself before, Caitlin, but now I know I came to find you.'

She drew his face down to hers and kissed him on the mouth, allowing her love unrestrained expression. He held her tenderly and kissed her, softly at first and then with increasing urgency. They lay back in one another's arms, each rejoicing in the other's closeness as though it was a homecoming.

Caitlin lay for a long time against Jonathan's chest, hardly moving, listening to the sound of his heart beating as though it kept her alive too.

'You know I've loved you all these years,' he said.

She propped herself up on one elbow and smiled at his shy confession. The moon peeped in between the curtains as if she had a right to witness this meeting of true lovers and to bless it.

'Do you think you could marry me?' he asked. 'English by birth, Irish in love and Scottish by superstition—a funny mixture, aren't I?'

'I think,' replied Caitlin, 'that you're just about perfect.'

And the lady in the moon smiled knowingly.

Pack this alongside the suntan lotion

The lazy days of summer are evoked in 4 special new romances, set in warm, sunny countries.

Stories like Kerry Allyne's **"Carpentaria Moon"**, Penny Jordan's **"A new relationship"**, Roberta Leigh's **"A racy affair"**, and Jeneth Murrey's **"Bittersweet marriage"**.

Make sure the Holiday Romance Pack is top of your holiday list this summer.

AVAILABLE IN JUNE, PRICE £4.80

Mills & Boon

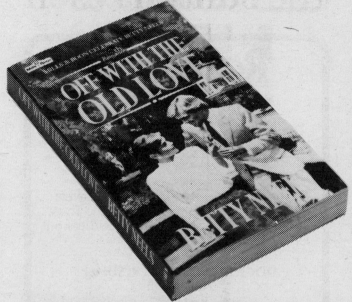